The Meadow

—— A Novel ——

SCOTT A. WINKLER

The Meadow
A Novel

Copyright © by Scott A. Winkler, Ph.D.

Authored by Scott Winkler, Ph.D.
Prepared for Publication by Travis J. Vanden Heuvel

Published by Peregrino Press, LLC
2284 Glen Meadows Circle
De Pere, WI 54115
www.peregrino.press

Cover design by Travis J. Vanden Heuvel.
Cover photo © Peregrino Press. ALL RIGHTS RESERVED.

ISBN (paperback): 978-0-9993574-2-2

This title is also available in electronic and audiobook formats.

Printed in the United States of America

Portions of the chapter "November 18, 1967" appeared August 5, 2016, in *Peninsula Pulse* as "The Hunt."

Portions of the chapter "July 3, 1969" appeared August 4, 2017, in *Peninsula Pulse* as "Chicken."

I would like to acknowledge the outstanding work of my editors, Bethany Michiels, Lizzie Costello, and Sandee and Taylor Richey. Thank you for the time and dedication you've invested in *The Meadow*.

I would also like to thank George Clark, Kristie Hamilton, Liam Callanan, Andy Martin, Rachel Buff, Sheila Roberts, John Goulet, Ed Risden, Genevieve Winkler, Grace Westphal, Katie Waege, Rebecca Rozz, Sandra Lucht, and Travis Vanden Heuvel for their support, guidance, wisdom, and encouragement.

It's a good day. Every day is.

— Scott A. Winkler

For Tom and Martha

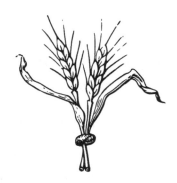

Prologue: April 6, 1958

CLAY AND I didn't need alarm clocks to wake us.

Our parents were still in the barn, milking, enabling our covert search for Easter baskets. We were supposed to wait until our parents came back to the house. Our mother, Anna, loved watching us search as much as we loved finding the baskets, but we could never wait. Every year, we found them early and ate from the assortment of sugary treasures; not enough that our parents would notice, but enough to appease our sweet tooth before putting the baskets back in their hiding places to satisfy our mother.

Clay had always been far better at basket hunting. He possessed instinctive abilities, which led to his munching jelly beans or foil-covered chocolate eggs before I caught a whiff of mine.

Some years, he found my basket first, and the only thing that kept him from digging into my stash was my being a year older—not that I'd have roughed him up or given him an Indian burn to teach him a lesson. Clay was nearly my size, and the times we had tussled, he'd more than held his own before our father, Otto, pulled us apart.

That Easter, though, I beat him at his own game. My basket had been tucked away behind the 21-inch black-and-white RCA in the corner of the living room, and it contained more than just Fry's Crème Eggs and Whoppers and Marshmallow Peeps; atop the usual haul of candy was a baseball glove, tied closed around a baseball with strips of a flour sack towel. "Check this out!" I called to Clay, who was peering behind the couch.

He reached me in three steps, landing on his knees as I pulled off the cloth strips and slipped my left hand into the mitt. It was a bit large, but I didn't care. I spread my fingers, flexing open the glove, and grabbed the ball with my right hand. I brought the glove close to my face, breathing in the earthy-sweet scent of leather and the neatsfoot oil generously applied to the palm and pocket. I squeezed my fingers inward, and the glove closed easily. "Lucky!" Clay said. "But if you got one…" He was already back to searching, too busy to finish his thought.

I studied the glove. It was stamped with an assortment of labels: "Rawlings LB10" on its heel, "Lew Burdette" and "Deep Well Pocket" on the palm, and "World Series Champ" in the pocket. I felt ten feet tall, remembering how the previous year, my father, Clay, and I had listened to Earl Gillespie on the radio, broadcasting the Braves' long march to their seven-game triumph over the

Yankees in the World Series. I'd never known our father to be anything but a serious man, but when the Braves won, I saw him smile in a way I'd never seen; it was warm and surprising, and that Easter morning, it came back to me as I slapped the ball into the pocket, snapping the glove closed around it.

I heard Clay's "Yes!" from the mudroom off the kitchen and ran to see him kneeling on the stone-tiled floor, slipping his hand into his own glove and slapping the ball into the pocket as I had. In our excitement, neither of us bothered to eat any candy. Instead, we moved from room to room, pounding our fists into our new gloves and imitating the radio calls until our parents came in from the barn—and we realized that we'd forgotten to return the baskets to their hiding places. Our mother's face drooped with disappointment, but before she could voice displeasure, our father spoke up with the day's second surprise: "It's okay—I think the boys can be forgiven, no? It looks like you found something special in your baskets?"

As Clay and I finished each other's thoughts with ever-increasing speed and volume, our father winked at our mother and her disappointed look disappeared. We ate a quick breakfast before our parents returned to the barn to finish morning chores. Clay and I washed up and got dressed for church so that our parents could do the same when they returned to the house. We made quite the sight in our Easter suits as we stood in the living room for the picture our mother took each year—Clay in his three-button brown woolen coat with high lapels, me in a blue pinstriped jacket and vest, and the pair of us with our new Lew Burdette signature model gloves on our left hands. We still wore the gloves when we climbed into the back seat of the car next to our grandmother for the drive into Gillett for the late service attended by the farm families at St. John's Lutheran Church. "*Was ist das?*" Grandma asked. Clay and I repeated our dueling reportage for her. What we said may not have meant much to her one way or another, but what she picked up in our voices made her smile. She placed her arm around my shoulder and pulled me close. I felt her strength even though her hand was missing one finger and part of another, lost to a threshing machine years earlier as she helped my grandfather harvest oats. "*Du bist ein guter Junge, Walter,*" she said.

"*Danke*, Grandma," I said. I leaned into her hug and breathed in the floral scent of her perfume.

The gloves didn't leave our hands until our father insisted we take them off and leave them in the car before going into the church. Having worn it almost non-stop since finding it earlier that morning, my hand felt naked without the mitt. Clay and I both fidgeted through the service. It didn't matter that all the stops were drawn on the organ or that the congregation sang full-throated versions of "Christ the Lord is Ris'n Today" and "A Mighty Fortress is Our God"; it didn't matter that Rev. Stubenvoll thundered from the pulpit in the tones he reserved for church holidays; nor did it matter that our father reminded us fidgeting boys impatient to get back to their new baseball gloves would be sent to visit "The Church Man" in the basement—something that we didn't realize, until we were older, was the clunking of the boiler in the furnace room, not the tragic punishment of rowdy children in a dungeon.

The gloves went back onto our hands as soon as we returned to the car, and they stayed there until we sat down to Easter dinner shortly after getting home—though I kept mine on my lap during the meal. My mother had put the ham and her scalloped potatoes into the oven to bake low and slow before she and my father had milked the cows that morning, and by the time we returned from church and she placed the entire meal on the table—my grandmother's potato rolls, bowls of green beans and carrots they'd canned the summer before, the dense, rich black forest cake for dessert—the ham was falling off the bone.

Though it was all delicious, and though we ate more than our fill, Clay and I couldn't get away from the table fast enough. Upon being excused with a nod from our father, we dashed to our bedrooms, lost our Easter suits, and jumped into clothes more conducive to the moment we'd anticipated since finding our baskets.

The day was cold. The yard was still frozen in patches, soggy in others. Most of the snow had melted, with the exception of the dirty banks on either side of the driveway, dwindling with the slow advance of spring. We didn't care about the cold or the brown lawn or anything else. Clay and I felt nothing but excitement as we began tossing the ball back and forth. I couldn't believe how easy it was to catch with my new glove, my first glove. Clay and I had both used the old, cracked monstrosities we snagged from the bucket at Apple Orchard School, beating the older boys to them from our spot near the coat rack in the school's single room, but they were nothing like the glove I wore that day. In my mind, Clay and I became Red Schoendienst and

Johnny Logan, Eddie Mathews and Joe Adcock, Henry Aaron and Del Crandall, Lew Burdette and Warren Spahn. We re-enacted the radio calls as we remembered Earl Gillespie having intoned them, the weak springtime sunlight transformed into the August glow in our cheeks.

Our game moved throughout the yard, back to the orchard behind the house where the branches of the apple trees were still bare, to the expanse between the box elder that shaded the house in the summertime and the corn crib filled with ears from last fall's harvest. It finally wound up in the side yard. As we passed by the front porch, our father stepped out to tell us we'd need to go to the barn for our afternoon chores in five minutes. Clay sprinted back toward the old outhouse, and I stood by the lilac bush. Our long tosses arched through the air, and after each throw, we took a step closer to one another.

As we drew closer, our tosses leveled out and sped up. Clay's arm was impressive. Even as a first grader, he threw faster and more accurately than the older boys during our improvised games at recess. His throws to me that day were crisp, some even popping in my glove as I caught them. And as the distance decreased and velocity increased, the time between throws shortened, each of us seeking to get the ball out of our gloves and back to the other as quickly as possible.

We continued in that manner, each exchange drawing us closer and closer until no more than ten yards separated us. Clay grinned. I was proud of handling his precise throws. Some of the boys at school couldn't. Some didn't even try, fearing the consequences should their reflexes prove inadequate. Clay made things more challenging for me; rather than delivering the ball at chest level as his throws had arrived with mechanical regularity, he started picking his spots: one at my knee, the next at my ankle, a third at my forehead. I knew from the look in his eye that their placement was intentional, though I couldn't tell if his glimmer of satisfaction came from my being able to handle his throws or from his being able to target body parts apparently at will. I'd like to believe it was the former.

His final throw was the only one I didn't catch cleanly. I'd just snagged a low throw an inch above the brown blades of last summer's grass and slung it from the same bent-low position. Clay's return throw was so rapid that I didn't have time to set myself. The ball caught me in the chest, and for a moment, it took my breath away. Clay looked surprised, but he said nothing as our father came out to the porch. "Time for chores," he said.

For a moment, I couldn't breathe before the cold rush of April air violently filled my lungs as I retrieved the ball from where it had rolled. Neither of us spoke as we went into the house. As I changed in my room, I lifted my t-shirt and studied the spot where the ball had struck me. A red welt was growing just to the left of my sternum. I could even see the faint stitches of the ball on my skin in a darker, more severe red. The mark would become a bruise by the time I took a bath that night and metamorphose through various shades of purplish-green and yellow in the days ahead. The bruise hurt for a week and remained sensitive to touch beyond that, but the mark would endure.

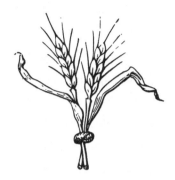

May 27, 1968

IT WAS GILLETT'S Memorial Day Parade, and my father led the VFW honor guard. The rich baritone of his voice called cadence to the veterans of Korea, World War II, and even two survivors of the First World War, limping down Main Street, their chests swollen and spines as straight as they could muster given the injuries they suffered and the slow march of time.

Though I couldn't see them behind me from my position in the back row of the band, I heard them. And while I knew some of the men behind me struggled to march the route given their injured joints and missing limbs, I was having troubles of my own. The horn had never been such a burden. I'd shouldered that sousaphone in more performances and parades than I could count, but that day, the curved brass of the instrument cut through the cream overlay and black jacket of my marching uniform. I imagined an indentation forming in my deltoid and staying there for weeks. Maybe the doctor conducting my physical at induction would take one look and declare me unfit. *"4F, son. DBS—disabled by sousaphone. Now get out of here. Don't hold up these other fine Americans."*

The local draft board would soon meet, and without a college deferral, my number would be drawn sooner than later. That prospect had dogged me for months, and with the draft board's inevitable notice looming, I'd entertained thoughts. I read things. I knew what young men in my circumstance sometimes did.

My father couldn't have fathomed that. World War II had been his war. He'd served in Europe in 1944 and 1945. Beyond such basics, however, I couldn't have related any of the particulars of his service. Those sparest of details were all he shared, despite his unapologetic patriotism and his insistence that my brother Clay and I serve our country as he had served. That insistence had brought me to the verge of blows with my father more than once and had taken me down a precarious path through my private hell.

That Memorial Day, his voice sliced through the rolling snares of the drum line, and at my father's command, I heard the honor guard pull back the bolts on their rifles, a synchronized, mechanical sound that gave me chills. That day, I pictured eighteen men loading blank cartridges into the chambers of their guns, pictured them simultaneously close the bolts on their magazines, pictured them firing as one into the air, a half-beat after my father's command. And that day, I winced at the reverberation of their shots burning through the lacquered brass of my instrument, something alive and malicious, something that sought to harm with impunity. Momentarily, I thought my knees would buckle, the sousaphone no longer a musical instrument I loved to play, but an immense yoke I shouldered. I kept marching, though, lifting and laying down my feet, checking my diagonals and spacing, struggling, but never missing a beat as we marched past the storefronts, their windows decorated with all manner of red, white, and blue streamers and bunting, and past the light poles, each of them adorned with vertical banners extending above the curb and proclaiming "Gillett Welcomes You."

The report of the shots died between the buildings on either side of Main Street and left me anxious. Their concussion rose a gorge in the back of my throat that flooded my mouth with a flavor situated somewhere between iron filings and lemonade. I should have loved marching with the band that day. Music had been one of my passions throughout high school. The parade should have been memorable for things other than the weight of the horn, but I'd been carrying too much for months: My Lai and Tet, the assassination of Martin Luther King, Jr., Cronkite's nightly body counts, and fantasies of escaping to Canada had accumulated atop the stress of finishing high school, my father's expectations, both stated and implied, and the options Mr. Grzesch and I had discussed. Some burdens I carried by choice, the rest by circumstance, and the specific gravity of it all had caught up with me that morning, making my feet cinder blocks I willed to walk the streets of my hometown.

The drum major's whistle cut through my father's commands, through the drum line's cadence, through the heft of the sousaphone slicing into my shoulder. Two long and four short chirps brought the mouthpiece to my lips, and we played a brisk, street-marching version of "God Bless America." I'd first memorized the piece freshman year, a standard spectators took to heart as we marched past. Those sitting in folding lawn chairs or on blankets spread over the sidewalks rose to their feet at the first strains. Children who'd scrambled to retrieve candy tossed from patriotically-themed floats and flat-bed trucks stopped in their tracks at their parents' prompting. Men removed their hats and women placed their hands over their hearts. Even deaf Dickie Miller stopped pedaling his bicycle along the route and stood at attention, imitating the spectators.

Their sincerity was admirable. My fellow townspeople's genuine pride motivated them to respond in that manner. It wasn't merely the obligation of ceremony and custom. To them, such gestures held meaning, and I couldn't help but feel something in kind. Admiration, pride, appreciation—but disappointment, too; I embraced the scene even as my stomach churned.

I heard the cheers from either side of the street, and I pictured the VFW Honor Guard behind me in lock step, dressed identically in their navy pants, crisp white shirts, and blue caps with embroidered gold piping. I pictured my father's stern decorum even as he swelled with pride at having fought and served. I couldn't resent that pride, neither my father's nor that of the other vets. I'd already tried that. Nor could I begrudge the acknowledgment and thanks given by the people along the route. What I couldn't understand was their acceptance of Vietnam as a good war and their willingness to put me and others in harm's way without question. Gillett had already lost three young men in the jungles of Vietnam, the three young men who would be honored after the parade. I'd gone to school and played ball with those three, had played in the band and baled hay with them, but rather than prompting questions over the motives for and necessity of Vietnam, their deaths had only strengthened the town's collective resolve that America's objectives were noble. And most disillusioning of all, their deaths had done nothing to weaken my father's resolve that I take up a rifle in service to my nation.

The band turned left onto McKenzie Avenue in front of St. John's Lutheran and its imposing clock tower, leading to the end of the parade route—Veterans' Memorial Park, a half-block span of grass and flowers built around a vertical slab of gray granite with plaques bearing the names of Gillett's sons who'd made the ultimate sacrifice in the first and second World Wars, in Korea, and, as would be unveiled for the first time that day, the Vietnam War. At the park, the band stood in formation as Rev. Stubenvoll delivered an invocation and Mayor Lambrecht offered bland but heartfelt opening remarks.

The band then played "America the Beautiful." As we played, I watched the back of Meg's plumed marching helmet three rows ahead of me, dipping and rising as she breathed and played her trumpet. I thought of our post-parade plans—a picnic at our most special place and an evening together given my leave from chores and milking. I thought of the graduation gift I'd hidden away for Meg and wondered how she might receive it. My stomach stopped churning, and the weight of the sousaphone lightened for the first time that day. The Meg effect.

The clouds in my thoughts didn't disperse, however. They hadn't all spring; the sun sometimes poked through, but even when Meg and I were together, wisps remained. I noted the irony of the unsung lyric "home" as we ended the piece, and I caught a glimpse of Mr. Grzesch. He was a beat poet dropped into a Norman Rockwell painting. His long hair stood out from the crew cuts and close-cropped, Brylcreemed styles favored by other men, and his attire, an untucked bright yellow and green paisley shirt, frayed, torn jeans, and worn leather sandals, separated him from the pressed khakis, stiff polyester dress pants, and simple geometry of shirtsleeves around him.

I wanted to find fault with this ceremony and display, but I couldn't. Nor could I embrace it. My head and heart were duking it out, and neither held the upper hand. Mr. Grzesch clapped his hands as the rest of the crowd offered the mayor polite applause, but I knew him better than that. I remembered what he'd told me about Mark Twain and petrified opinions.

Mayor Lambrecht's voice was tinny over the public address system as he again spoke. "Ladies and gentleman," he said, "we gather every year at this time and in this place to remember those sons and fathers, brothers and uncles and cousins and friends from our little corner of this great land, those who have made the ultimate sacrifice to give us the gift of living and breathing freely in these United States." The crowd interrupted his speech with applause—equal measures obligatory and earnest. As the applause dissipated in the blue May sky, I was grateful for my sousaphone, still heavier than usual, and the excuse it afforded me for not joining them. I also believed in the importance of honoring sacrifice, but the names being revealed that day—and the thought of my name or my brother's one day being inscribed on a memorial plaque—held me back. I'd graduated from high school a day earlier and didn't savor knowing that my draft notice would arrive sooner than later. I didn't savor knowing that I'd much prefer to attend college than to bust my chops in Basic before being shipped to Southeast Asia. I didn't relish knowing that my hopes and dreams played second fiddle to the ambitions of men in high places. And I especially didn't appreciate the thought of leaving behind my family, my home, or Meg and the future we'd sketched out for ourselves—a good future that was supposed to begin with our attending the University of Wisconsin together and stretch on from there. I watched her in the trumpet section. I wasn't surprised to see that she hadn't joined in the applause either. Meg was very much her own person, and neither decorum nor the sway of numbers would compel her to act in a manner she didn't embrace. She looked back over her shoulder and found me. From beneath the brim of her marching hat, her brown eyes spoke. *It's going to be okay, Walt.* For the first time that morning, I smiled.

Mayor Lambrecht shifted at the podium and shuffled papers, a pleased look on his face. "As I look around me, I see my family, my neighbors, my fellow citizens, and as I see each and every one of you, I am compelled to remember that the freedoms we enjoy, the freedoms that allows us to live as we do, come with a price." He cleared his throat. "I'm especially reminded of that fact when I think of those no longer with us today. They're the ones who paid that price. Today, I am proud to offer thanks to three more of our sons—Herman Woerner, Ronnie Gilbertson, and Mark Raddatz—whose names I now reveal for the first time on our town's memorial to the fallen." The mayor stepped away from the podium, gingerly grasped the sheet draping the plaques on the marker, and pulled away the shroud.

With its removal, the VFW Honor Guard again followed my father's command. Seven of its members fired blanks into the sky, re-loaded and fired again, re-loaded and fired a third time. The late spring foliage of the trees dampened the concussive volley of gunshots, but not before they sent a shock through the brass of my sousaphone for the second time that day, a vibration that passed through me in an instant and was gone. This time, it left me feeling touched by something foreign and new and abhorrent. At our band director's cue, Meg raised her trumpet to her lips and began playing "Taps." Her notes that day were rich and round, their tone possessing a weight made all the more palpable by the muffled sobs of the families of the newly fallen veterans whose names were etched in bronze not yet weathered by the passage of the seasons.

As I bore witness to those families' mourning, the weight returned, pressing down on me. I knew the sons for whom my neighbors wept and felt something catch in my throat. For the second time that day, I swallowed hard, forcing it down, refusing to be swept away. From my spot in the band, as Meg's final notes rose toward a sky so blue it hurt to look at it, I couldn't help but notice ample space on the marker for additional names.

May 27, 1968: Afternoon

MOST OF THE people attending the memorial service departed for the annual city-wide picnic that kept Main Street closed to everything but foot traffic each Memorial Day, but a few people lingered—family members of the fallen whose names were on the marker. I couldn't bring myself to leave right away either. I kept my head down and tried to be as inconspicuous as possible with a sousaphone encircling me. Eileen Ehlers, who'd been my fifth grade teacher, traced the letters of the name of the son she'd lost north of the forty-fifth parallel in Korea, and Mark Raddatz's parents stood a few feet away from her. I'd once had an art class with Mark. He'd been three years ahead of me in school, but he'd taken me under his wing. He became a big brother of sorts during my first season of high school ball and even invited me to his graduation party. Mark's father shifted uncomfortably from one foot to the other, his hands jammed tightly in his pants pockets, and his mother looked to the ground, her forehead resting in the L of her thumb and index finger, her right elbow braced against her torso. I felt their pain, and for an instant, I wondered how my family would react if my name or Clay's were ever to be preserved on the memorial.

A hand pressed against the middle of my back. Meg. I knew her touch even through the uniform. "Ready, Tubaman?" she asked quietly.

I cast a final glance at those still there. "Let's hit it."

We made the short walk from Memorial Park back to the high school and turned in our marching uniforms for the last time. I packed away the sousaphone, and we said our final good-byes to Mr. Pelow, who'd resurrected what had been a moribund band program prior to his arrival four years earlier. "We'll miss you," he said. "It's not easy replacing musicians like the two of you." Mr. Pelow, though not much older than Mr. Grzesch, was a large man with a receding hairline. Fine beads of sweat stood out from his forehead, and he dabbed them with a white towel from the improvised workbench tucked in a corner of his office. "Please stay in touch," he said, offering each of us a heart-felt, if clammy, handshake.

Meg and I exited through the back door near the band room and walked to my parents' car. My father had given me leave of chores and access to the car for the entire Memorial Day weekend. He could be that way—stern taskmaster with high expectations, but he and my mother willingly shouldered extra work if it meant making something special possible for Clay or me. I opened the passenger-side door of the sky-blue '62 Plymouth Fury. Meg slipped into the seat and lightly ran her fingernails over my forearm, raising pleasant goose bumps.

We drove to Meg's house, an old Victorian her father had made his labor of love whenever he found time outside of his duties as Superintendent of the Gillett Public School District. From the wide palette of colors he'd used to paint the trim to the restored scalloped siding he'd installed on the turret, the entire house reflected not only pride of ownership but also the full range of skills he'd shared with students as a shop teacher before becoming an administrator. That work had also earned him the respect of people in Gillett; desk jobs received a measure of esteem in my hometown, but people whose sweat resulted in something tangible enjoyed the greatest admiration.

Meg and I stepped through the front door into the foyer of the Eiseth's home. Her mother called us to the kitchen. When her husband had accepted the superintendent's job, the open home economics position became hers, part of a package deal for the district. Mrs. Eiseth had made lemonade for Meg's outing with me. "Trying to steal my man's heart, Mom?" she asked.

"You've already found your way there and didn't have to go through his stomach." She set the plaid-patterned, push-button Thermos next to the picnic basket Meg had already prepared.

"Thanks, Mrs. Eiseth," I said.

"You're very welcome, Walter." She smiled. I wondered if, when Meg was older, she'd have the same smile lines as her mother. Thoughts of growing old with Meg. Less weight.

"Give me a minute," Meg said, moving toward the stairs. "I'm going to change."

"If you take too long, your father and I just might bring Walter with us to the doings on Main Street."

"Dream on, mother," Meg said. She flew up the stairs.

"The band played well today, Walt," said Mrs. Eiseth. "Fine tuba playing as always."

"Thanks," I said, "but Meg was lights-out."

"She's okay," Mrs. Eiseth deadpanned. "Warren and I are going to miss hearing her practice up in her room." Mrs. Eiseth paused. "We're going to miss you, too, Walt."

I shrugged. "That's awfully kind of you. You've been good to me. I'll always appreciate what Mr. Eiseth did for us with Mr. Grzesch."

Meg's half-humming, half-singing came down from her room: "A Day in the Life" from *Sgt. Pepper's*. "Warren's not afraid to go to bat for people when it's justified," Mrs. Eiseth said. "He wouldn't have hired Tom Grzesch if he weren't exceptional, and he wouldn't have approved your and Meg's independent study with him if he hadn't seen how you could all benefit."

"Still," I said. "Studying with Mr. G…" I couldn't find the words.

"That's why we teach, Walt." She turned toward the open window above the sink. "Warren?" she called into the backyard, "are you almost ready?"

"Coming, coming," he said, his reply somewhat muffled. So many people had been in my corner over the years, in so many ways, making my father's insistence of his vision for my future all the more frustrating.

Meg entered the kitchen like a whirlwind. Meg's entrances, be they in a kitchen, a classroom, or anywhere, made people feel her presence. She exuded life and brought an energy that filled the room. It wasn't by deliberate effort on her part, though. Her presence simply was. She wrapped her arms around my shoulders. "I hope Mom hasn't bored you to tears."

"I could really use a nap," I said, stretching and feigning a yawn.

Meg gave me a quick slug on the shoulder then stepped away from me to twirl her sundress. "Wow," I said, "that beats a marching uniform any day!"

"I should hope so," she said. "I've been saving this one."

"Well worth the wait," I said.

Our walks to the meadow and the time we spent there gave Meg and me time to simply be us. We didn't have to try to impress anyone. We could laugh at how my lips trembled during our first kiss beneath the beech tree. We could spread a blanket and watch the slow sway of wildflowers in the breeze or pluck wide blades of grass and try to outdo one another's shrill whistles. Many of our discussions about the future had taken place in the meadow. There, we sensed that what we shared was deep and real and good, as certain as the cycle of seasons.

Memorial Day marked our first visit of 1968. Partly, our absence had been due to the endless procession of low-hanging clouds that spring, dressed in gunmetal gray, and their accompanying rainfall. Nothing of Biblical proportions, but they were cold and frequent enough to keep us indoors, unlike the previous summer when we didn't have to worry if the sky opened up and soaked us to the bone, when warm days turned into languorous nights as clouds parted, stars dotted the sky, and moonlight silvered everything around us, making the meadow itself a work of art.

Classes that spring had also conspired with Mother Nature. Rather than letting up on us because we were approaching graduation, teachers had buried us beneath a procession of projects and exams: a twenty-minute presentation in history on a major campaign from World War II, comprehensive exams in chemistry, multiple tests in advanced math.

And then there was Mr. Grzesch's capstone for Meg and me to round out our second year of independent study with him. We each composed a twenty-five page paper on the relative health of the American Dream, typed, double-spaced and footnoted, incorporating at least a dozen outside sources—works of fiction, poetry, drama, non-fiction, and criticism applicable to our moment. Even though we'd begun the marathon at the beginning of the semester, the final weeks felt like a sprint completed while we were running on fumes.

The end result, though, was worth it. Partly, the success of our work was due to a perfect storm: LBJ and Westmoreland and Richard Nixon and Ho Chi Minh and a Summer of Love and a thousand other things established the backdrop for the questions Mr. Grzesch posed and the answers we developed through the lens of great works. Partly, it was due to Meg and I fueling and motivating each other; we were competitive, each of us wanting to outperform the other while working to help each other achieve our goals. Partly, it was due to words and ideas mattering to us. And of course, it was due to Mr. Grzesch, who encouraged inspiration and perspiration in equal measure and was either too young, too foolhardy, or too wise to envision any limitations on what we could accomplish.

But all that was behind us. The drive to the meadow from Meg's house was short, just ten minutes. We parked where the railroad tracks intersected with 4 Towns Road rather than beginning from the farm as we typically did. I didn't want to go through formalities with my family and risk my father saying something that would bring back that morning's feelings. I simply wanted to give myself over to the Meg Effect as soon as possible. We unpacked the trunk of the car—the picnic basket, the lemonade, the blanket we'd spread beneath the beech tree so many times before, Meg's denim tote trimmed with floral fabric, and the graduation present for Meg I'd hidden in the folds of the blanket. I also grabbed the well-worn anthology of poetry in which we'd dog-eared the passages we most liked when reading to each other.

As we walked along the tracks, I tried to capture moments: the sun on Meg's hair, the green canopy of leaves, the liquid warble of a robin, the feeling of Meg's fingers laced between mine. I wanted to record each of those moments indelibly on the canvas of my memory. *I'll need them soon*, I thought. When Meg squeezed my hand, the images of the Raddatz family and Mrs. Ehlers, the echoes of ceremonial rifle shots, and the imagined weight of cinder blocks dropped away.

We took our time, pausing often, sometimes to identify shapes in the clouds dotting the sky—a mischievous alligator stretching open his jaws as an unsuspecting rabbit lolled nearby, or a cat curled before a fireplace glowing with the light of the midday sun. Before Meg, I'd not known I had the capacity to locate such spirits in the sky; it wasn't the only part of myself she'd helped me discover. We paused for Meg to pick the flowers she wove into her hair as she joked about how we might freak out our parents by telling them we were running off to join a commune. We stopped on the trestle spanning the mouth of Christy Brook as it spilled into Spiece Lake and played Pooh Sticks with broken branches dropped from the trees on either side of the track bed, a game she'd taught me courtesy of her affinity for A.A. Milne.

Seeing the meadow from the tracks took some effort now that the trees had leaves. The first time I'd seen the meadow, I was a young boy, checking the *herrlichkeit* with my grandmother, and she veered off the tracks down a narrow path that took us to the opening, the same path Meg and I took through the mixed hardwoods between the tracks and the meadow. Meg and I walked through dappled sunlight, and when we emerged from the trees, our jaws dropped. Our meadow was cloaked in an expanse of daisies. Stems, graceful and strong, branched and branched again, each topped with flowers whose bright yellow faces were fringed with snow-white petals. A stand of daisies had grown there the summer before, but nothing resembling the ocean now stretching before us, and so much sooner than it should have appeared.

"Wow," I said.

"Wow," Meg whispered, her voice reflecting her sense of awe. "This is…"

"Amazing," I said.

"Ours," Meg said. She rose on her toes to kiss me. I felt the same thrill I'd felt with our first kiss in the meadow, but this kiss also had another quality, something deeper, something older. When we came up for air, the swaying sea of daisies seemed to approve.

"Ours," I agreed.

Instead of going directly to the beech tree, we walked the periphery of the meadow, as though disturbing the flowers might have broken their spell. When we reached our tree, I spread the blanket, careful to tuck the small box holding Meg's present beneath one corner, closest to where the smooth gray bark of the trunk disappeared into the soil.

"We made it, Walt," Meg said as she sat down.

"We did," I said. We both knew she meant more than simply graduating. We'd been together for twenty months. We'd pushed each other. We'd completed a course of study with Mr. Grzesch whose rigor and expectations I wouldn't again encounter for years. We'd arrived at a point where either of us could raise an eyebrow, purse lips, or tilt a head and simply *know* what the other was saying. Meg had stood by me through my struggles and still believed in our future. And I'd stood by Meg as she went through her own trials; while her parents didn't drop the hammer of authority in the manner of my father, they were less than approving of her decision to go to college to become an art teacher, a vocation that didn't sit well with the former shop teacher in her father and the home economics teacher in her mother.

A switch had tripped when Meg and I drove away from Gillett High School after the parade; until that drive, though I said, grudgingly, that I accepted the post-high school cards I'd been dealt and was okay with my circumstance, I hadn't begun to feel anything close to matching what I was telling myself. I still wasn't happy with the hand the Fates had dealt me, but acceptance had begun, however tenuously, to take root.

As Meg and I ate at the foot of the tree, we re-lived commencement. She loved receiving her diploma from her father, and I recalled my own sense of satisfaction when I spotted my family in the third row and saw my father's pride in me. Such displays were rare for him, and when they did happen, they reminded me there was more to him than a narrow-minded sense of entitlement to determine my future; they gave me hope.

We ate our fill, and as I leaned back against the trunk of the tree, Meg rested her head against my chest. I wouldn't have been surprised if she'd tried to tickle me (she did it well, her own unconventional way of showing she cared without having to resort to words), but she didn't that day. She lay there, silent for several minutes as I sensed the hum of the invisible flywheels whirling in her head. Finally, she spoke. "You're good for me."

"It goes both ways," I said.

"You know better than anyone the demands I make on myself—and from others. I know I'm not always an easy person, Walt. I can ask a lot of people. But you listen to me. And you care. That sounds so simple but," she closed her eyes and swallowed, "but it's not. You make me a lucky girl, Walt. I just wanted to say 'thank you.'" Meg sat up and reached into her large denim bag to remove a package she handed to me. It was wrapped in a rich burgundy paper that creased slightly between my fingers as I held it. "It's for you," she said.

I opened the flap and let the paper fall away, leaving a picture frame in my hands. In it, beneath glass, was a painting that she'd done of the meadow from the perspective of our entry point, a spot-on image of the late September day I'd first taken her there. Her brush strokes had animated the native grasses and the yellow coneflowers that had survived the first frost, captured the oranges and yellows of the changing leaves and the texture of the bark of the trees in the foreground, re-created the reach of the beech tree's limbs over the northern fringe of the meadow. I wanted to say so many things, but all I could manage was, "God, Meg."

"Good," she said. "And there's one more thing." She gently took the painting from my hands and turned it over. "Recognize this?" she asked, gesturing to a passage that had been inscribed in Meg's flowing cursive on the heavy paper stapled to the back of the frame.

I did. Meg had written the closing sentences of the first formal essay I'd composed for Mr. Grzesch before we began our independent study—the piece about the meadow and my grandmother, the one for which Meg had been my peer reviewer and which prompted her to not-so-subtly invite herself on our first walk to the meadow. "I'd had my eye on you from the first day of school," she said, "and when Mr. Grzesch made us partners, I was as scared as I was excited. I was even more excited when you read your piece to me in class."

"You're easily pleased," I said.

"You're talented, but it's more than talent. I knew it from that essay." She squeezed my hand. "Do something for me?" she said. "I love it when you read beautiful, smart things to me—especially beautiful, smart things you've written—so could you read what's on the back?"

I couldn't deny Meg's request. She pushed the buttons that made me feel good. I cleared my throat, blinked back the sting in my eyes, and began reading: "On those walks, my grandmother had far more in mind than exercise or teaching me the names of wildflowers or enjoying time with her grandson—though each of these were undoubtedly elements of our sojourns. I'm now old enough to realize that checking the *herrlichkeit* is more than surveying fields and forests and meadows. It's what brought her and my grandfather to America, to the Midwest, to Gillett, Wisconsin. The *herrlichkeit* was their dream. That dream prompted her to take five year-old me by the hand and plant the seeds now growing in my soul. I still walk those paths even though my grandmother died four years ago. Those walks sustain her dream, nurture it, keep it alive in me. Someday, I hope to check the *herrlichkeit* with someone who means as much to me as I meant to my grandmother, someone with whom I may dream and sow seeds that yield a bountiful harvest."

As I finished reading the words, Meg spoke. "I love you, Walt," she said.

"I love you too," I said. We'd said those words before, but that day, they possessed a physicality entirely their own.

Taking a deep breath, I reached for the gift that I'd tucked beneath one corner of the blanket. "Remember camping on the Apostle Islands last summer?"

Meg grinned conspiratorially. "Ditching my parents for a couple of hours the last day was especially fun."

"Yeah, that was alright," I replied with a straight face while feeling the same rush that had helped us fend off the chill wind that had rolled off Lake Superior. "Do you remember going through the stones on the beach of that small island?"

Meg nodded. "I still have some of them up in my room."

"Me, too," I said. The image of Meg on the beach flashed across my mind. She was wearing an old pair of jeans and a denim jacket, her hands sifting through the mix of sand and stone. She'd never been afraid of getting her hands dirty. "There was one in in particular I found that afternoon."

"And you've been saving it?" Meg asked.

"For you," I said, handing her the box.

Meg held the box in her palm opened the lid. "Oh, Walt." She removed the necklace from the box. A Lake Superior agate dangled from a slim sterling chain. She cupped the stone and studied the agate—a deep crimson nugget the size of a thumbnail that seemed to glow from within. Concentric white bands spread from a single point at the heart of the agate, and the entire stone had been buffed to a soft luster. "You found this?" she asked.

"I did," I said. "Here." I brought the ends of the chain to the back of her neck and fastened the clasp. "Just before your parents paddled into view, I was picking through several stones, but this one was different. When I looked close, I could see the banding, the depth of color. I remembered Mr. Baumgart sharing some very cool stones in freshman physical science, and this one reminded me of the Lake Superior agate in his collection."

I described sensing a triangulation between her, the stone, and me, how I brought it back home to show my great uncle, who devoted much of his spare time to collecting and categorizing rocks and minerals. He confirmed my suspicion that it was a Lake Superior agate and offered me ten dollars for it, but the horrified look on my face prompted him to withdraw the proposal. Instead, he offered to put it through his tumbler, buffing and polishing the stone. From there, I'd taken it to a jeweler in Shawano, and with the cash I kept in a Folger's Coffee can in the back of my closet, I bought a setting and had the agate attached to a sterling silver chain. I'd originally planned on giving it to her for Christmas, but something told me to wait.

Meg listened to my story, occasionally glancing down at the stone and letting it dance over her fingertips, and as I finished, I felt my heartbeat increase in speed and intensity. "Meg, I'm not getting down on a knee here, but I want you to understand that I'm making you a promise."

She let the stone rest on her chest, just above her heart, where it rose and fell with her breathing. "I'm listening," she said.

"For months now, you've been trying to take away my anxiety. You've told me, more than once, that I'll come home in one piece, and that you'll be waiting for me, that we're strong enough to make it through anything thrown at us." I paused and breathed deeply. I'd gone over the words I wanted to say a thousand times, but they escaped me.

Meg took my hand. I felt her fingers tremble, but her touch still calmed me. "It's okay, Walt," she said.

I swallowed hard. "So I want you to know that the agate, the necklace, they're my promise that I will come home to you."

Even when we were alone, Meg wasn't given to overt demonstrations of emotion, but she couldn't help herself. She wrapped her arms around me and we held each other close and tight. At first, our breathing was short and irregular as we each sought to control something welling up inside us, but it eventually grew measured. We kissed. I tried to convey to Meg just what she meant to me, in the pressure of my lips, the placement of my hands, the way I pulled her against me, and I felt the same from her.

When our kiss ended, I could tell from the light around us that the sun was nearing the horizon. The day that had started with such somber tones had been transformed. Meg looked at me and nodded. She slipped one foot out of her sandal and ran the arch of her foot over my leg. "Come here," she said, motioning me closer. "It's okay."

From my knees I moved closer to kiss her. Meg grabbed the front of my shirt and pulled me onto her. Her lips tasted like strawberry lip gloss. She opened her mouth to take my lower lip between hers; her tongue danced electrically.

We'd come close before, but each time, while the flesh had been willing, the spirit had been weak—sometimes for me, sometimes for Meg. Perhaps too many sermons had seeped into our brains.

Perhaps the not-so-subtle proclamations of our parents had worked as intended. Perhaps the fear of people talking should consummation produce more than intended held us back. But that Memorial Day, there was no doubt what we wanted there in our meadow, where we had begun, and what we shared beneath the beech tree was good and right and real and ours.

July 4, 1968

THE LIGHTS AT Mosling Field were an explosion of white against a summer sky bleeding pinks and oranges into indigo. That night, July 4, was the debut of night baseball for the Dairyland League, as our all-stars—my brother Clay and I among them—warmed up for the annual Door/Dairlyand All-Star Game between the best of the Door County and Dairyland Leagues. Clay and I had played on Mosling Field before, but being under the lights for the first time made me want to jump out of my cleats.

As Clay and I played catch along the right field foul line, our tosses gained velocity, the ball's trajectory causing it to hop as it sped toward its target. As my glove snapped closed around one of Clay's bullets, I was reminded of our games of chickenball when we were kids. We'd start at either end of the yard, a good 150 feet apart, and lob the ball until one of us asked the other, "You ready?" and received a "yup" in return, prompting the throws to begin in earnest. Even when we were young, when being Clay's senior by a year should have made me his athletic and physical superior, Clay's arm outclassed mine, and I witnessed it all too well during those chickenball games. With every step closer, we'd ramp up the velocity until eventually we were flinging the ball from positions close enough to allow us to smell the fear in each other until one of us could no longer stand it, chickening out by diving out of the path of the malicious sphere. More often than not, I was the brother who flinched.

But that July 4th, playing catch with my brother beneath the lights of Mosling Field, there was no flinching. Just a surreal calm that had followed the out-of-my-cleats sensation. All day, I'd been bouncing through an array of feelings. Pride that at having just turned 19, I was the second-youngest player (Clay being the youngest) selected to play in the annual contest dating back to 1919; satisfaction at my play having turned around since Meg and I made and celebrated promises on our Memorial Day picnic; nervousness at the prospect of stepping into the box against Door County's Freddy Richey, a southpaw who'd bounced around for years in the minors before and after his three-year stint with the Pirates in the late 1950s; and tranquility at feeling in my bones that I would make it through my tour of duty, buoyed by the knowledge that Meg would be there for me.

The one thing that should have been bothering me more than anything else, the fact that I now had a concrete date, August 1, to report to the Military Entrance Processing Station in Green Bay, had no effect on me. That, too, could be traced back to the meadow on Memorial Day. I'd gained a peace of mind I'd unsuccessfully sought since I started fretting the summer between my junior and senior years. My opinions of the war hadn't changed, and the one-two punch of Gene McCarthy's failure and Bobby Kennedy's assassination did nothing to suggest that an end was in sight. Knowing, though, that Meg and I had begun our life together had done more for me than any amount of reading or rationalizing could accomplish, no matter how powerful or persuasive the text, no matter how nimble the mental gymnastics. *We* were certain.

I had not, by any stretch, adopted my father's perspective regarding service to my country. I still believed opportunities for service existed outside of toting a rifle or sloshing through jungles on the other side of the globe, but I no longer felt compelled to push his buttons, nor did he seek to push mine. My fear of returning stateside in a flag-draped coffin had not entirely dissipated, but it had become as manageable as such fear could be; I'd come to believe the odds of my coming home alive had infinitely improved given something definite to come home to: joining Meg in Madison, the GI Bill, becoming a teacher cut from the same cloth as Mr. Grzesch—these prospects, too, were real, definite, certain. The unspoken truce in the long-running war with my father over military service had brought a peace to the Neumann home that we hadn't known in some time. Clay and I weren't feeling the turbulence that had been ever-present during our daily chores and the simple routines of living under the same roof, and my mother had actually begun to smile again.

My performance on the diamond since Memorial Day was gravy. I'd done a poor job of manning second base and a worse job of hitting during what should have been my best season of high school ball, but my play for Gillett in the Dairyland League had earned me the starting position at second base in the All-Star Game. As I trotted onto the field, I felt better than good. The air was alive—the buzz of the crowd, the crisp floodlights filling the night with luminescence, the anticipation of a good ballgame, the pre-game rituals of catch and pepper, the ceremonial first pitches and the National Anthem—and when I took my place at second base, my limbs were loose and my movements fluid. I glided to scoop a grounder tossed by the first baseman as our pitcher, Willie Spreeman of Breed, warmed up.

Willie, whose day job was delivering mail out of the post office in Suring, was a knuckleballer. I'd played against him the last two summers and was happy to play behind him that night; I knew all-too-well how he could make a hitter look pathetic. His pitches came to the plate with a tantalizing slowness that gave hitters the impression they could hold off on committing to swing until the last moment—and that's when the ball would dart or dive or dip, defying the laws of physics to leave the hitter desperately trying to adjust his swing. He set down the best Door County had to offer in one-two-three fashion each of the first three innings. Only one ball came my way, a lazy pop fly in the top of the second that landed softly in the pocket of my mitt.

We didn't fare any better against Door County's Richey. He

hadn't pitched professionally for several years, but he could still bring the heat, and experience had taught him how to keep hitters off-balance. In my at-bat against him, he lured me to crowd the plate before dancing me inside with chin music that drew good-natured boos from the partisan crowd. Having successfully backed me off the plate, Richey froze me with a sweeping sidearm curve that caught the black for strike three and ended our inning.

Door County's offense came to life in the top of the fourth when Green Valley's Lee Bergsbaken took the mound. Happy to see something other than knucklers, Door County's hitters jumped on the earliest offerings in the strike zone. A leadoff single was followed by a double to put runners in scoring position. The third hitter was a tall glass of water from Bailey's Harbor named Schartner. He jumped on Bergsbaken's first pitch, sending a towering shot to left that hooked foul inches away from the pole. I glanced at Clay before the second pitch. He positioned himself at the edge of the outfield grass and several feet closer to third base than normal. Having played alongside Clay for so many years, I knew to trust his instincts, so I wasn't surprised when he made the best defensive play I'd ever seen him make. After three straight balls, Bergsbaken grooved the 3-1 pitch. Schartner made full contact, sending a liner screaming at eye level toward the hole at short. Our third baseman, guarding the line, couldn't have made a stab at the ball had he wanted to, but Clay launched himself, his body parallel to the ground, his glove hand extended backhand. He snared the ball in the fringe of his glove's webbed pocket, a single-scoop vanilla cone, and as he fell toward the outfield grass, he tucked his shoulder and half-rolled, half-flipped so that he popped into a seated position facing third base, plucked the ball from his glove, and zipped a throw to our third baseman, doubling off the runner before he realized the ball had been caught.

It happened so quickly that I never left my crouch, my feet spread wide, my arms still a semi-circle dangling toward the infield dirt. My jaw went slack as the crowd rose to its feet. The players in this game were the best of the best in the two leagues, but only my brother, the youngest player in the contest, could have made that play. I shook my head and scuffed the dirt with my cleats. We may not have always gotten along with one another, but Clay was a thing of beauty to watch on the diamond and I couldn't help but feel pride. Clay was nonplussed. He casually rose to his feet, slipped off his glove beneath his right arm, and adjusted his cap before signaling two out to the rest of the infield.

Bergsbaken threw two quick strikes to the next hitter, both on the inside corner, before throwing his third pitch well outside. The Door County batter had no business swinging, but he did, lunging so that the bat actually escaped his grip. Somehow, he made contact. The ball looped toward shallow right field. I immediately broke on it, my cleats digging into the soft infield dirt as I raced toward the right field grass. The spin of the ball kept it slicing and slicing toward the right field line, as though it were sentient, intent on eluding me. As I tracked the ball, my world went silent. Like Clay, I launched myself. Like Clay, my body was parallel to the ground, slicing through the damp nighttime air. Like Clay, I extended my glove to intercept the trajectory of the ball. I know I didn't look as fluid or graceful as my brother, but in that moment, I felt perfect and beautiful, every bit the player Clay was, the player gnarled men champing at unlit cigars and writing in tattered notebooks had begun scouting that spring from the rickety bleachers of the town and high school ballparks where we played. And as my own trajectory yielded to the pull of gravity, the ball came to rest in the pocket of my mitt just before I collided with the earth and skidded along the grass, my glove hand inches above the turf to indicate to the umpires and everyone else that I'd made the catch, the kind of play that Clay made routinely, but which for me felt as rare and precious and worthy of preservation as Lake Superior agates and afternoons with Meg in the meadow.

As I pushed myself up, sound returned to my world as though piercing a gauzy wrap—the applause of the crowd, the soft thuds of my fellow All-Stars trotting for the dugout and offering their congratulations. As I began my own trot off the field, I found Meg in the stands, four rows behind the home dugout, her face flushed, her eyes flashing. She was wearing the same sundress she'd worn Memorial Day and the agate necklace. I felt something like warm honey spread through me. Her parents were there, too. Mr. Eiseth wore a look of genuine delight, and he tipped his hand toward me as though indicating a bow; Mrs. Eiseth had let, however briefly, her always proper decorum give way to shout. Even my parents were there—a rarity as their work on the farm typically kept them from attending more than a couple of Clay's and my games each season. My father pointed toward the field, his finger alternating between Clay and me as he turned his head and spoke to the spectator on his left. I knew he was praising us, something he was quick to do for anyone who'd listen, but something he withheld from us as though offering approval would make us soft or make him suspect as a father. My mother's expression was one of delight and confusion, as though she wanted to offer a whoop and a holler but couldn't reconcile that impulse with her instinct not to call attention to herself. And Mr. Grzesch was there, too, his hair even longer than the mop he typically wore during the school year. He smiled, his hands pressed together as mirror images of each other, and offered a brief nod. I loved the man for so many reasons, and his own love of baseball only strengthened that sentiment.

In the dugout, Clay sat next to me, assuming his customary position—glove on the bench to his right with a ball nestled in the web of the pocket, cap off and atop the glove, and bent from the waist toward the field, the better to study the opposing pitcher and note defensive alignments. I leaned against the back wall of the dugout, enjoying the sensation of my lungs expanding as I breathed deeply, the faint aroma of cut grass combining with the thought of Meg's perfume as I imagined it wafting into the dugout, a combination of lilacs and spices. Lee Bergsbaken made a point of walking past us to offer a terse "thank you," curt and low and under his breath—a surprise coming from him as he was generally regarded as the surliest player in the circuit.

"Wonders never cease," said Clay, his eyes glued on the Door County pitcher warming up. He was scheduled to bat third that inning.

"Hell of a play you made," I said.

"Attention to details," he said. That was Clay in a nutshell. Little things mattered to him—and to me, for that matter—that others may overlook, but his points of emphasis weren't mine, reflecting his character just as my particulars reflected mine. I played baseball because I loved the game, its place in history, its mythical and literary qualities, even in high school; Clay loved the game, too, but for him, the science of the sport made all the difference—the lines and angles, the physics, the tendencies of particular players in particular situations. His God-given talents made him good; attention to detail made him great.

"Still one hell of a play," I said.

"Yours wasn't half-bad either," he said, turning back from his forward-leaning posture. For a split second we made eye contact, and I saw something resembling warmth. It was a departure from his customarily stony veneer, and I noted the significance of his understated compliment; like our father, Clay wasn't quick to offer them, and when he did, you could rest assured they were well-deserved.

We rallied in the bottom of the seventh. Our lead-off hitter walked, and our second hitter advanced him to third on a long single to right-center. Clay then ran the count to 2-2. The Door County pitcher, despite the men on, continued working the corners, trying to force Clay's hand. Protecting the plate, Clay fouled off six straight pitches before the pitcher caught just a bit too much black. Clay roped the ball, a liner that never rose more than ten feet above the ground but struck the base of the right field fence, 315 feet from home, on the fly. The right fielder, who'd been playing Clay to pull, lumbered toward the ball as it

caromed into foul territory near our bullpen. Clay was fast. He'd
been the fastest player on every team for which we'd played, and
he ran that night like a poem, his legs a rapid verse rounding
first and slanting toward second on a route that lessened the
angle of his path to third, where he slid headfirst to cradle the
bag half a heartbeat before the third baseman slapped the tag. I
cheered along with the crowd from my spot in the dugout and
watched Clay calmly rise to his feet, hold his hand up to call
time, brush the red infield dirt from his uniform, and flip his belt
outward to empty the soil that had gathered there as he plowed
through the earth on his slide. Though he'd covered some 270
feet of base path in what felt like a heartbeat, he didn't breathe
heavily; he stood there, right foot on the dirt, left foot on the
bag, knee slightly bent. From my vantage point, Clay appeared
to stand higher than anyone else on the field, and for a moment,
the lights played a trick on my eyes, bathing my brother with
an aura, the younger of the Neumann brothers glowing like a
baseball god. It's an image I carry with me—Clay standing on
third after his seventh inning triple—an image I need; the others
hurt too much.

We pushed five runs across the plate that inning, the last of
which I brought in with a sacrifice fly to center field, and the
mood of our squad was upbeat as we took the field in the top of
the eighth. Even Clay demonstrated a bit of levity as he threw the
ball to me in its final trip around the horn. He glanced back over
his shoulder, toward center field, where just over the horizon, the
glow of the July 4th festivities at Gillett's fairgrounds bled into

the blackness of the night. "If we make quick work of them, we just might be able to make it back for the fireworks," he said. Clay had loved the fire department's annual show from the time he could walk—one of the few things that could get to drop his poker face for a few minutes as he stared into the night sky with a sense of wonder.

"I don't mind fireworks myself," I replied, looking at Meg in the stands. Suddenly, I was ready for the game to end, and our manager brought in just the man to make it happen. Delbert DeBauch of Pulcifer took the mound, a quirky submariner whose odd delivery kept the ball hidden from batters until the instant it left his hand, which seemed to miss scraping the crown of the mound by no more than a whisker. He changed speeds, and his pitches darted and dove, generally inducing those fortunate enough to make contact to send grounders to the infield.

Door County's lead-off hitter, a scrappy second baseman named Lautenbach from Jacksonport, had other ideas. Our third baseman, a big farm boy from Suring, apparently hadn't noted the way Lautenbach ran out his previous at-bats—sprinting to first on both of the walks he'd drawn, a la Pete Rose. He played back, and Lautenbach dropped a bunt. By the time our third baseman barehanded the ball, Lautenbach had already crossed first.

Clay and I shifted into double play position as the next hitter came to the plate. We were counting on our pitcher's bread and butter to set us up for a play that Clay and I could have turned in our sleep. We'd been turning double plays since Little League. I glanced at Clay to confirm that I'd be covering the bag with a right-handed hitter up, but I saw him again looking over his shoulder toward center. Even Superman had his Kryptonite. "Clay," I said, "it's mine."

My short bark caught Clay's attention and brought him back. He nodded. DeBauch threw two quick strikes before the hitter fouled off the next two offerings and drew a ball. On the sixth pitch, the hitter sent a grounder to the hole at short. With his range, Clay had no problem reaching the ball, and as soon as the hitter had made contact, I broke for second. It should have been textbook, 6-4-3, except that somehow, a page had been torn from the text. In feeding me the ball at second, Clay lost his grip. He double clutched making his throw, causing me to remain planted at the bag for a moment that stretched far longer than that.

Lautenbach had been off on contact. By the time Clay's throw reached me and I began my pivot, Lautenbach was barreling into second, rolling toward my legs with a high slide designed to break up the play in a manner that would have made Ty Cobb smile. I don't remember the ball spilling from my glove, but I will always remember the explosion I felt in my left knee, as though one of the invisible boomers that shook the night sky in honor of America's freedom had been planted and detonated in my joint. I landed on my back, and my head snapped against the ground. Darkness dropped like a blanket three times. Initially, it was a momentary loss of consciousness, a fleeting dusk that promised to return as I teetered on the edge of perception; then, it was the night sky above me, soon occupied by teammates hovering like phantasms draped in wool orlon, the first of them Clay. His typically flat expression had been transformed, his eyes wide and his features contorted in an odd mix of shock and pain. He dropped to his knees, his lips moving much faster than the words reaching my ears, as though they traveled through air that had become thick and liquid around me, a garbled "God, Walt, I'm sorry. I'm so sorry." Finally, the world slipped away entirely as unconsciousness swaddled me like an unforgiving quilt.

July 5 – 6, 1968

I AWOKE, BRIEFLY, to the glare of hospital lights.

I couldn't speak, just mumble unintelligible sounds that didn't seem to come from me. The white noise of the emergency room came to me through the same liquefied air I'd sensed at Mosling Field, a wash of suction and beeps overlaid with the hum of fluorescent light tubes that cut through on a frequency entirely their own. My teammates had been replaced by looming hospital personnel, weird, masked caricatures wearing scrubs garish shades of green and blue, their mouths covered by masks that undulated with the movement of their lips. Their words didn't register. I felt someone squeezing my hand, but the sensation was quickly replaced by flames radiating from my left knee. An intense red-orange flared behind my eyelids before being replaced by an inky blackness.

When I next awoke, the room was dim. My head throbbed in counterpoint to the dull ache in my knee, as though the pain threatening to explode was being held in check by a dam ready to crumble should whoever held his finger in place decide to shift his weight. An IV tube snaked from my wrist to a bag of clear fluid hanging over my right shoulder. My mother was sitting in the chair next to the bedside table. "Mom?" I said. My tongue was thick and reluctant, my mouth pasty. I tried sitting, but I couldn't raise my torso. When I tried to push myself up, my arms were uncooperative, and I fell back to the bed with the same sensation that had jarred me when I landed on my back after falling down the hole through which we dropped bales from the haymow in our barn. I groaned and didn't try sitting up any more.

"Walt," my mother said. "Shhh." She rose from her chair, setting a book on the bedside table and coming to my side. She placed one hand on the rail of the bed and the other on my forearm. Her fingers were icy, but they warmed as she gently stroked my arm.

"What...?"

"No talking." Her voice was a blend of stern reprimand and the warmth she exuded whenever Clay or I were under the weather or had suffered even a scraped knee or unsightly bruise. She pushed a button on a hand-held box sitting on the table. "I just called a nurse. You're in the hospital—"

"Hospital?" I asked.

"Shush," she said. She leaned over and kissed my forehead. Even in the dimness, I could see her eyes were red-rimmed. "The hospital in Shawano. You're in intensive care. You have a concussion, and your knee is hurt, too. The doctor has to wait for the swelling to go down to know how bad it is."

I looked down the length of my body and saw my left knee bundled in elastic bandages, my leg suspended above the bed. A nurse soundlessly glided into the room. "Thank you Mrs. Neumann. Hi, Walt," she said. "I'm Kendra, and I'll be taking care of you overnight. If there's anything you need, just push that button," she said, nodding toward the box my mother had used. "We need to keep you here in the ICU a bit longer." Her voice seemed to come from further away than her position relative to me, but her words and lips at least matched up. My mother's warm hand rested on my arm as the nurse repeated what my mother had told me and checked the chart hanging at the end of my bed. "You're almost out of the woods, Walt," she said. "24 hours is the magic number. We should be able to move you into a room of your own in the morning."

ICU? The memories of the All-Star Game came back to me in flashes. Lautenbach rolling into me, my knee exploding, my head snapping back against the infield dirt, Clay standing over me... and he'd said something. The nurse had mentioned 24 hours, and fragments of my life clicked into place like pieces of a jigsaw puzzle. My mother was here, but what about my father and Clay? Almost 24 hours. That would put them back at home, probably milking cows, finishing the evening chores. And Clay there on the field, his face contorted—had he apologized to me? And where was Meg? I imagined her father having to hold her back to prevent her from jumping over the fence and rushing to me. I wished she were there with my mother and the nurse. A word or a touch from her would have brought me more comfort than anything dripping through the IV.

Then my induction notice came to mind, the envelope on my dresser at home, and I felt a throbbing in the back of my head. The date for processing the newest cog in America's military machine was just over three weeks away, but my scrambled brain imagined an MP stationed outside my door, monitoring my status, ready to whisk me away to Basic as soon as a doctor proclaimed me fit.

"Walt," the nurse said, "do you need anything? The doctor will be getting into specifics with you and your parents in the morning, I'm sure—but can I do anything to make you more comfortable?"

I spoke, my words thick and slurred given the desert in my mouth. "Water?" I asked, followed by "Meg?"

"First one's easy," she said, smiling, bringing a cup of water from the table closer to me and tilting the straw toward my lips. I sipped from the straw, and when the cool water entered my mouth and spread over my tongue, its trail combined fire and reprieve, the shock of the iciness and the relief of the drought that had overtaken my mouth.

I continued drinking until I had to stop for breath. "Thank you," I said. My tongue felt nearly normal, my voice no longer reluctant.

"You're welcome," the nurse said.

"What about Meg?" I again asked.

The nurse looked to my mother, who mouthed "his girlfriend." The nurse nodded. "That," she said, "requires some patience."

I groaned. "How long have I been out?" I asked.

"You arrived in the ER around 9:30 last night," my mom said.

Kendra checked the watch on her wrist. "It's 7 o'clock right now. According to your charts, you briefly regained consciousness when you arrived at the ER, then slipped back, so it's been about 22 hours."

"22 hours?" I said. I became aware of a discomfort in my groin, a sensation that went beyond the fullness of my bladder. "I really think I need to go to the—"

"No getting out of bed for you just yet," the nurse said. "We've got things under control. A little uncomfortable down there?"

"Yes," I said, dreading her response.

"That's a catheter."

Bingo. I felt the blush in my cheeks, and my mother studied the floor tiles. My Grandpa Neumann had been hospitalized for three weeks before he passed; for the most part, he slept morphine dreams, but when he was awake and able to speak, his one complaint had been the catheter.

"But it should come out tomorrow," the nurse said. "Once you're in your own room, the doctor won't have your leg ratcheted up, and if you can handle crutches, which shouldn't be a problem for a strapping lad like you," she said, winking at my mother, "you'll be cleared for bathroom duty. Give the nurse's station a buzz and someone will come over to make certain you get there and are safely seated—"

"Seated?" I cringed.

"Or we could help you with a bedpan. Don't worry," the nurse said. "We're trained to look away."

Nice. My mom and a nurse sharing a laugh at my expense in the ICU—that could only mean, though, that her earlier news that I was out of the woods was accurate. The nurse continued, "We can't let you crash and burn." Her reassurance didn't alleviate my embarrassment, however. "Anything else?" she asked.

"When can I see Meg?" I asked.

"Right, Meg," she said. "She'll be able to see you during regular visiting hours, but I must advise you—nothing must interfere with your recovery."

"Mom," I said, hoping parental intervention on my behalf might defuse my sharp-witted nurse.

"She's the trained professional, Walt," my mother said. "What Nurse Kendra says goes." The two women exchanged smiles.

I realized, then, that in the space of a few minutes, my head no longer felt as though it were blanketed by one of my grandmother's quilts, and I'd forgotten about the pain in my knee. I hoped the pleasant buzz I was beginning to feel was the result of knowing that I'd soon see Meg, not an effect of the concussion or any pain reliever coursing through my veins. But as my mother and the nurse spoke in low voices, those induction papers and a looming appointment with Uncle Sam again came to mind. I'd seen the news footage that summer: of police dragging away young men who'd burned their draft cards, the stories on the case of Muhammed Ali, whose heavyweight championship belt couldn't hold off prison time. I'd chosen not to interfere with my appointed date, but I was worried nonetheless. I cleared my throat and spoke. "Nurse?" I asked.

"Yes?"

"No one's looking for me outside, right?"

The next morning, my entire family was in my new room, which featured large windows overlooking the Wolf River rolling by. I hadn't slept terribly well, even after my mother told me that my father had already called the recruiting office in Green Bay to inform them of my injuries, and when I did sleep, I had odd dreams of Muhammed Ali guarding the door to my hospital as Howard Cosell queried him about the Tet Offensive. Ali's braggadocio with the sportscaster was punctuated by his trademark rope-a-dope and crisp jabs and hooks into the air. The dream may have been prompted by my concussion or by apprehension. Meg's promise had given me the mental resolve to answer the call that had come with my draft notice. That resolve hadn't erased every anxiety, though; promises, made or implied, have always meant something to me, so my resolution to report bore weight as well. Uncertainty killed me.

"Well, Walt," my father said, "you're looking a heck of a lot better than you were when they carted you in here." He sat in a chair, leaning forward, wringing his hands. He made his best effort to smile. When he did, creases extended from his eyes, and it occurred to me that I'd never before noted the depth and expanse of those wrinkles.

"I guess I'm feeling better, too," I said, "but I can't really say I remember a whole lot about getting here." I was relieved that I had proven capable of transporting myself from bed to bathroom on crutches, though the trip there and back—just six feet from my bed—had left me more than a little tired and triggered a dull throbbing in both my head and my tightly wrapped knee.

Clay sat in a chair he'd backed into the corner nearest the window, where he looked back and forth between me and the river outside. He fidgeted, as though sitting were difficult, and something in his eyes told me that he had much on his mind that needed to be said. The odds of that happening weren't terribly good, however, especially with my father in the room. Getting Clay to open up at any time was as difficult as pulling a breeched calf from its mother as she freshened—the calf's life may be at stake, but necessity is no guarantee that the efforts will be successful.

"That was...quite the play you made the other night," my father said. "You and Clay both." He looked at my brother, who was still looking out the window. "Same inning." Compliments were a big deal for our father. He was struggling to offer what amounted to effusiveness for him. I'd never been able to figure out why he had such difficulty commending us directly but had no problems doing so to others.

"Thanks," I said, my own brief reply feeling more than a little awkward. "They were. Clay's was better, though," I said. I pictured him parallel to the ground, pursuing the liner, but the image was quickly replaced by the one of him standing above me, apologizing.

"Aww, Walt, they were both terrific," my mother said. "We'll remember them for a long time, won't we?"

"They were something, alright," my father said. When had he decided to become so vociferous? Even though he'd played some ball during his youth, he'd never taken the game as seriously as Clay and I did, and I doubted he and the rest of the crowd that night could've appreciated what Clay had done to even make the play possible.

The most unusual thing I noticed about my father that day, however, were the dog tags he wore, dangling just beneath the V of his button-down shirt, but flashing momentarily when he reached up to let them dance over his fingertips before letting them drop to his chest. I had never seen him wearing the tags— had never even seen the tags, period. For all his patriotism and dedication, for all his high-minded principles about obligation and service, he was reluctant to bring personal experience into the picture, even when he had the occasion to do so. In the past year, in the midst of all our quarrels and debates, he'd had ample opportunity to punctuate his points with details of his own experience in World War II, but he never delivered more than the basics—Europe, 1944, commendations locked away in a footlocker buried beneath winter coats upstairs—and my mother never breathed a word of it.

My father's earnest but awkward efforts at compliments ended when two doctors entered the room. The first, a neurologist named Dr. Tietyen, reassured my parents that while my concussion was serious, I didn't face immediate danger. He told us that over the next two months, I should lay low as much as possible, that staying out of the summer heat and avoiding bright light should bring me a degree of comfort and promote recovery. He also told us that while headaches likely wouldn't be uncommon, they shouldn't become debilitating. The time I'd spend in the hospital in the days ahead, he explained, would be important for monitoring me and ensuring that precisely such a problem didn't appear. And finally, Dr. Tietyen advised avoiding strenuous physical activities over the next couple of months. "Though from the looks of that leg," he said, "that shouldn't be too much of a problem." We asked about any other possible long-term effects, though I'm certain my father was coming from a completely different angle than I was; I didn't want to imagine a blow to the life of the mind, couldn't imagine a life without ideas, especially after I'd been awakened to such a world by Mr. Grzesch over the last two years. Dr. Tietyen reassured me that the concussion shouldn't have any effect on mental functioning or capacity. We all breathed sighs of relief for our own reasons.

The second doctor, an orthopedic specialist named Dr. Burgess, said that he still needed the swelling to go down in my knee before he'd be able to operate and see the extent of my injury. He anticipated finding any of a number of problems, likely more than one—torn anterior or medial cruciate ligaments, torn meniscus. "You're certainly not going to be playing any more baseball this summer," he said, "and next summer might even be pushing it."

My father shifted in his chair. The doctor noticed this and said, "I'm sure, though, that a strong, young man like your son, Mr. Neumann, will be able to rehabilitate the knee with a fair degree of success. Will it be as good as new? Not likely—your son is probably going to know when rain is on the way for the rest of his life, and there are going to be days when he will welcome aspirin and hot or cold compresses, but his knee, with work, will get to the point where he can play ball again. You might, Walt, want to consider a position change, though. I've seen you play in the Dairyland League over the last couple of seasons. My son plays for Cecil. You hold down a good second base, but the outfield may be much friendlier to that knee."

My father could hold back no longer. "That's kind of you, doctor, but it's not his playing ball that concerns me," he said, rising from his chair to stand at my bedside. He held the rail of the bed next to my knee, still wrapped in compression bandages and surrounded by large bags of ice. My father looked at my knee and shook his head. "Walt has certain obligations, doctor—he's already received his papers."

"Mr. Neumann," Dr. Burgess said, "at this point you may not want to—"

My father cut him off with the kind of steely glare that, when I was younger and less stubborn, had immediately ended any protest or disagreement. The last year had toughened me, however, and my father's old tricks didn't affect me in the same way they did the uninitiated. I looked down to where my starched hospital gown lay across my thighs. "Want to what, doctor?" my father asked. "I've raised my sons to believe in duty and obligation." *Good God,* I thought, *here it comes.* I knew the buttons that, when pushed, prompted righteous indignation. Dr. Burgess had brought his fist down on a big one. "Walter and I have butted heads more than once over the last year about his future plans," he said, his face growing a deeper shade of crimson, "but he has recently come to understand the dignity of answering the nation's call." *Call it what you will,* I thought. "When he can get a doctor's clearance," he said, "I'm certain that Walt will be only too happy to honor his obligation to America."

Up to that point, I hadn't bothered trying to explain my reasons for agreeing to respond to my draft notice. Accord alone was all that mattered to my father, and if it helped him sleep at night to think we'd found common ground, I would give him that—and give my mother some peace before I left home. I couldn't, and wouldn't have wanted to, imagine how he would have responded to my telling him that Meg and I making love and promises beneath a beech tree at the meadow gave me the peace of mind to soothe my fears and overrule my conscience. I wouldn't burn the card and beat a path for Canada or remain stateside but go incognito, attempting to elude authorities. Someone like Muhammed Ali may not have been able to become invisible, but a tuba-playing second baseman from a dairy farm in Wisconsin, with a degree of smarts, might have been able to make it work for a while, at least. And for as appealing as either of those options had seemed at various times, I couldn't entirely escape the uneasy feeling they gave me when I considered them in earnest. Meg's promise had given me something more tangible.

I bit my tongue as my father staked his claim to speak for me. When he finished, I opened my mouth, but Dr. Burgess beat me to the punch. "Mr. Neumann, I admire your, and presumably your son's, patriotism." His voice was firm, but the gradual ascension in its tone combined with the precision of his inflection showed that he intended to decisively nip any diatribe in the bud. "But no matter how deep-seeded and well-intended those convictions may be, they will never restore your son's knee to a state that a physician would approve for active duty in any branch of the United States military. I'm sorry."

My father's face went from crimson to ashen in a heartbeat. My mother said nothing, though I could see her thoughts racing. Clay stopped looking out the window. He turned to look at me and shake his head.

My independence day.

"I won't—?"

"It's...?" My father's voice trailed off and he swallowed hard. He placed his hand on the bedside table to steady himself.

"As I said," Dr. Burgess continued, his voice now softer but still measured and authoritative, "we won't know the extent of Walt's injury until we actually go into the knee, but even in a best case scenario, the joint has been seriously compromised." He paused and lowered his clipboard, doing his best to explain the repairs he anticipated making. Though I tried, I couldn't entirely focus on his explanations of ACLs and MCLs and the shock absorbing qualities of meniscus, on his extrapolations regarding incisions and their effects on my knee. I was too busy trying to wrap my mind around the freedom I'd craved most when it appeared that my future would be determined for me by generals and politicians and draft boards who hadn't an inkling of what they jeopardized by putting me into fatigues with a rifle in my hands. "Three things I can definitively say, though" Dr. Burgess said. "One, after surgery, we'll immobilize the knee with a cast. Two, you won't be putting any weight on that leg for a couple of months, minimum. And three, no doctor in his right mind, even one bankrolled by the Defense Department, would clear you for duty."

At that declaration, my father shuffled unsteadily toward the door, moving as though he were no longer acquainted with his legs, his mouth partially open as though he expected words to spill out of it, though none came. Clay was close behind him, having sprung to his feet and brushed past the doctors without so much as an "excuse me." My mother's head was on a slow pivot. She watched the other two Neumann men leave the room, turned to me, then back to the door. She raised her right hand to her face, her fingertips framing her open mouth, and looked back at me again. For a moment, her look of concern melted, and I saw in her eyes a glimpse of what I felt. She knew, and I sensed her happiness—happiness for me, happiness for herself, too, as I would later discover. But the recognition was fleeting, replaced by the knowledge that her husband and other son needed her at that moment. She leaned forward in her chair and looked at me. "Walter, I—"

"I know, Mom," I said, smiling. I placed my hand over hers where it grasped the rail of my hospital bed and squeezed, hoping my warmth would find her and stay with her. "Go."

She leaned over to kiss my forehead before leaving the room, but not before thanking the doctors, using both of her hands when she shook theirs. Knowing my mother, those squeezes conveyed worlds more than her words.

I turned to the window in my room. I hadn't noticed the sun prior to that, and I noted that the river's current was especially swift that day. I imagined it running toward the dam near the paper mill, where the water would continue running toward the Fox River and eventually spill into Lake Michigan. But while the river waters ran swift that day, the sunlight was steady, spreading a soft, fixed shimmer over the moving water, which reflected the light back through my window to briefly dance upon the ceiling as though laughing at a private joke.

July – August, 1968

THAT MORNING'S LUMINESCENCE dancing on the
ceiling had lulled me to sleep. When I awoke, Meg was
standing at the foot of my bed, the Lake Superior agate resting
just beneath her collarbone. She was frozen in space, breathing
in fits and starts between laughter and tears. She placed her hand
on my leg as if she feared I might break.

"It's okay," I said. "Everything's okay." I raised one arm, motioning for her to come to the head of the bed. She took my hand
and leaned in to kiss me. Strawberries.

"Ahem." An exaggerated cough interrupted our moment. It
was Mr. Eiseth. Mrs. Eiseth stood beside him, cradling a vase of
daisies. "Hello, Walter," she said. "How are you?"

Meg stood so that her parents could see me. "I'm much better now," I said, looking at Meg.

"Oh," Meg said, letting go of my hand to bring the flowers to my bedside table. "We checked first," she said, "but even if they'd said 'no,' I would've found a way to get them here."

I knew. Meg the unstoppable. "When?"

"Just this morning," she said. "Being there without you felt odd, but I wanted to bring something that's ours."

"They're perfect," I said.

"Good," she said.

Meg's parents asked about my condition, and I shared what I could remember of the doctors' diagnoses, saving the best for last—Dr. Burgess' declaration—though I spared them the tension in the room and my father's and brother's abrupt exits. Meg said nothing as my words sank in, and her parents looked shocked before looking at Meg and then each other. Mr. Eiseth's lips moved beneath his mustache as he whispered something to his wife and she nodded. I'd never opened up with them about my fears and anxieties like I had with Meg and Mr. Grzesch. I knew, though, that Meg had shared my feelings with them, and they trusted Meg and I were more than high school sweethearts.

"So this means college sooner than later, Walt?" asked Mr. Eiseth. He spoke carefully, measuring his words so he didn't suggest an inaccurate read of the situation, but he couldn't conceal a note of satisfaction.

"That would seem to be the case, sir." Hearing myself speak those words made my new circumstance all the more definite, and I briefly wondered what my father had said to my mother when she caught up with him and Clay.

Meg looked at my leg. "So how are we going to get you hobbling around campus?" she asked. Though an artist, she'd also inherited a measure of the tinker in her father, and I knew she was already calculating ways of improving upon the standard crutch for my benefit.

I hadn't even had time to consider the question of college. Mr. Eiseth speculated that I wouldn't be able to go to school that fall, but that given the timetable for getting back on my feet, I should be able to begin classes second semester. "That will give Walt time to recover sufficiently while he applies and gains admission," he said. "Walt's record speaks for itself, but I'll speak with some folks I know in admissions and student aid." My father had forbidden me from so much as completing a college application; I hadn't shared with him that I had completed the application anyway but hadn't sent it in, fearing that word of my guidance counselor sending transcripts might leak in our small town.

I blushed with embarrassment and appreciation. The Eiseths came from a different world than the one in which I'd been raised; while my father looked at the world and saw things as he believed they should be, Mr. Eiseth seemed to see things as they could be and asked, "why not?" I first came to know that trait when he backed Mr. Grzesch's campaign to teach Meg and me independently, and it was on display again here in my hospital room. I loved my parents and my hometown, sometimes in spite of themselves, but for a long time, I'd found myself questioning them, questions whose answers—and lack of them—infuriated me.

I couldn't have known the price those answers would exact.

After two weeks in the hospital, I was relegated to home for a month-and-a-half. Dr. Tietyen had declared my neurological functions normal by the end of the first week, though he emphasized the importance of laying low and avoiding physical activity to allow for my brain's recovery from the concussion. At that point, Dr. Burgess opened my knee. When his suspicions were confirmed—torn anterior and medial cruciate ligaments and torn meniscus—he repaired the injuries according to the standard protocol of the time. Compared to the work of other orthopedic surgeons, Dr. Burgess was a Michelangelo.

The cast on my leg ran from the middle of my thigh to my ankle. As I hobbled about the house on crutches, I kept an unwound wire coat hanger with me so that I could get at the inevitable itches that reminded me of the scene in *Adventures of Huckleberry Finn* when Huck and Tom are waiting to prank a sleeping Jim. Unwilling to move and risk waking Jim, Huck begins to itch everywhere—except he can't scratch for fear of disturbing their target, which drives Huck crazy. Beneath the cast, it sometimes felt as if itches migrated when I sought to relieve them, and even the deftest maneuvers of the coat hanger couldn't get at every one of them.

Generally, I was a good patient. I was glad, though, to disobey Dr. Tietyen's directive against activities that could strain my eyes (and consequently, my bruised brain). Namely, for me, that meant reading. Reading was one of the two beacons that helped me survive being homebound that summer. The other, not surprisingly, was Meg. The books kept my mind alive, and Meg made me feel alive. During one of Meg's hospital visits, I shared my concern that the concussion might impair the gift I valued most, one my parents had unknowingly nurtured by example, and which Mr. Grzesch had fostered so artfully over my last two years of high school. She said there was only one way to find out. When I returned home, I started with Twain and moved on to Thoreau and Emerson and Whitman, voices Mr. Grzesch had introduced to Meg and me. My bedroom took on a Whitmanesque quality that summer: stacks of books and paper tumbling, spilling everywhere. My library had grown exponentially once Mr. Grzesch had introduced me to the wonders of used book stores, and I had taken to filling notebooks and legal pads with my thoughts.

Meg likely spent more time at my home that summer than her own. She was my best means of escape in a circumstance that felt like surreal confinement. Sometimes we'd talk about the books I was reading, or we'd read Emily Dickinson together. We relished her rebelliousness and expansive vision despite confining herself to the family home, and we loved the wry humor she deployed to expose the hypocrisy of the self-righteous. Sometimes, we bemoaned the Braves being in Atlanta and tuned in to scratchy broadcasts of Cubs games on AM radio. But mostly, we spoke of our future. Though we couldn't visit the meadow together that summer, we went there more than once, spreading our blanket on the floor of my room (door always open per parental dictate) or beneath the box elder in the yard, positioning wildflowers Meg picked before coming over.

During one of these picnics, Meg shared just how close she and my mother were growing. I was eating some of Meg's specialty—apple bread—when it occurred to me how much I'd miss it when she left for Madison at the end of summer. "Will you miss it more than me?" she asked.

"Close second," I said.

"Don't worry about it," she said.

"How's that?" I asked.

"I'm looking out for my man," she said.

"What do you mean?" I half-expected her to tell me she would invert the dynamics of care packages, sending loaves of her bread from school back to me. What she said next caught me completely off-guard.

"I've given your mom my recipe."

I couldn't speak for a moment. "Given it to her?" I said. "But I thought you only—"

"That's right, mister. I only share it with family."

Meg learned much from my mother that summer. They spent hours in my mother's two expansive gardens. They hilled and dug new red potatoes, picked strawberries, raspberries, peas, and beans. Later in the summer, they gathered kohlrabi, cauliflower, sweet corn, and broccoli. Some afternoons were spent in the shade of the box elder tree, podding peas, husking corn, or snipping beans, before freezing or canning the fruits of their labors. In the kitchen, they made pint after pint of jam: strawberry, raspberry, gooseberry, and currant. I loved the sound of Meg and my mother laughing together, loved seeing my mother looking at Meg like the daughter she didn't have, loved watching the two of them grow closer as they worked and laughed and learned and loved.

I saw little of my father and Clay during my recovery. They were both locked into the daily routines of the farm—including covering the tasks that had always been mine—as well as the draining work of baling hay and straw. Some of the lack of contact, though, must have been deliberate. Neither made a point of seeking me out, and when our paths did cross at meal time, my father had difficulty making eye contact with me. Any conversations, though civil, were blanketed by threatening clouds, and I felt that the right, or wrong, words would have prompted a downpour. At times, I almost missed the confrontations I had with my father earlier in the year, the feeling of aliveness that accompanied pulling no punches when each of us defended our positions with the kind of conviction true of our German roots.

Not surprisingly, I didn't know how to read Clay that summer. Like me, my brother possessed a significant inner life, but his was built upon a foundation far different and mysterious than mine. His loves, as far as any of us knew, were baseball, hunting, fishing, and his dream of one day joining the 101st Airborne. He worked diligently on the farm and passably in the classroom, and though he stayed out of the arguments between our father and me, his body language and facial expression clearly indicated which side he was on.

When Clay came home from twice-weekly games in the Dairyland League that summer, he immediately showered and made a beeline to his room, except for the night of August 10,

Gillett's final game of the season. Meg had already gone home for the night, and my parents had gone to bed. I was reading Ginsberg's *Howl* in my room, my window open should a night-time breeze decide to stir. The headlights from Clay's ride home came over the hill on our lane and flashed briefly across the far wall of my bedroom. Gravel crunched beneath tires as the car pulled up to our house. The car door closed with a solid *kachunk*, and the low rumble of the car pulling away faded as Clay's steps carried him to the front porch.

I continued reading. Clay, instead of grabbing something from the refrigerator and showering as I was accustomed to hearing, came straight upstairs, his feet on the steps an odd counterpoint to Ginsberg's ecstatic anger. But instead of turning to his room, Clay came to mine. My door opened quickly, a welcome *whoosh* of air momentarily chasing away the close humidity of August. Clay stood at the edge of the jamb, his feet shoulder-width apart, his arms thrust straight down toward the floor and his hands clenched in fists. His eyes reminded me of our father.

I didn't know what to say. The muscles in his forearms tensed, dancing beneath his russet skin, a stark contrast to the mottled whites of his fingers no longer balled into fists. I finally broke the silence. "So…" I said tentatively, "how did the game go tonight?"

Clay's brow furrowed, and I imagined a pressure gauge on his forehead, the needle climbing toward red. "We won," he said. The needle retreated from the red, but only a click.

"Good," I said, uncertain of what he'd say next.

The silence hanging between us was more than awkward. "I'm sorry," Clay finally said.

"Sorry?"

"Sorry," he said, "about your knee."

"What do you mean?" I asked.

"It was me," he said. "I botched it on the Fourth, the double play."

I half laughed. "It's okay," I said. "That night answered my prayers, Clay. Christmas in July. 'Independence Day' took on a whole new meaning." I missed playing ball, but I'd be going to college in January, not sloshing through the sweltering jungles of Southeast Asia. I'd be reading books for classes and writing papers for grades as I nurtured the life of the mind—not studying an infantry handbook to learn the fundamentals of my platoon's standard operating procedures and trusting proper field discipline to keep me alive.

I glanced down the length of my body. My white cotton t-shirt clung to my torso in the humid air. My right leg was bent at a 45-degree angle, climbing from beneath a pair of blue plaid boxers. My left leg was stretched out straight away from me, encased in plaster. I felt an itch beneath the cast, but I didn't reach for the reconfigured coat hanger at my side. "So I've got a bum knee," I said, "but it's on the mend. The cast comes off in September, and I'll be down in Madison come January."

Clay's firmly planted feet now shifted. He was struggling. "But still—I'm sorry that you're injured," he said, balling and unballing his hands, flexing his fingers. "I blew that play. I double-clutched. But there's more than that."

"Cut it out, Clay. It's okay. I mean, come on; we both know I never wanted—"

"That's just it." Clay cut me off. "What you want doesn't count for shit when your country needs you. It's like Dad's always taught us. I've taken away your opportunity—"

"My what?"

"To serve. Your opportunity to serve. I've taken that away, and I'm sorry."

Jesus Christ. "You've got to be kidding," I said. "Right?"

"I deprived you. By preventing you from fulfilling your obligation and doing your duty, I've done a disservice to you and to our country."

"You can't be serious." His words hadn't completely registered. I had difficulty processing his apology, if that's what it was, and I didn't want to follow whatever twisted line of reasoning had brought him to issue it.

"You haven't heard a thing Dad's taught us, have you?" Clay asked.

"Give me a break," I said, my voice rising. "The old man makes damn sure he comes through loud and clear, but that doesn't mean he's right. I'm not obligated to agree with him. Neither are you." Now that Clay had finally shown his hand, I didn't know whether to feel sorry for him or hate him; what I did know, however, was at that moment he should have been grateful that I still had a cast on my leg. If I hadn't, I'd have been on him so fast and hard that my blows that would have knocked him back to the Stone Age. I had to settle for flinging my coat hanger at him. Clay's reflexes took him out of its path, and the hanger struck the doorframe, gouging a jagged scar in the white-painted molding before it clattered to the hardwood. I heard my parents' feet hit their bedroom floor downstairs, then move quickly through the living room and kitchen.

"It's not that complicated, brother," he said. Clay was no longer flexing his fingers. He'd extended his arms, gesturing with open hands as though he pitied me, but something else was in his eyes, too. He'd crossed a threshold, had found his voice, and I'd lost any shred of hope that my brother might come to see things from my perspective. "The world's a rather simple place when you think about it: you farm and hunt and fish to put food on the table for your family; you stand up for what's right: democracy is good, communism is bad; you serve America when she asks because she gives you freedom—it's your obligation to defend the country."

The door at the bottom of the stairs opened, and my father's bare feet hammered the painted hardwood as he climbed the stairs. I groaned. I loathed the air of condescension in Clay's voice, how he embraced our father's perspective and parroted his lines. I loved them both, but at that moment, I tasted venom. I'd resigned myself to fate and rationalized that dreams were strong enough to protect and sustain me, but Clay's blunder ended the need to rationalize. It reanimated my dreams. My wish had come true, and if my knee was mangled, I didn't care. I cared even less that my injured knee deprived the United States Army of a grunt. The emotions Clay had revived were shredding serious psychological scar tissue, and their impact was only compounded by seeing my father behind Clay, his hair a mess and his face confused as he stood in the hall in his t-shirt and boxers, breathing heavily.

"What the hell is going on up here?" he said. He slipped

past Clay and into my room, standing between us, demanding answers sooner than later.

"Ask him," I said.

"Clay?" he asked, turning his attention to my brother. "What's your brother talking about?"

Clay still stood in the doorway, and his eyes shifted from the floor to me as he answered our father in a low voice. "I came by to apologize." My mother stood beyond Clay in the half-light of the hallway, hugging herself and wearing a look of trepidation.

"Apologize for what?" our father asked. I snorted, and he shot me a looked that would have stripped wallpaper.

"I caused Walt's injury in that game. It's been bothering me, and I never rightly apologized to him."

Our father frowned. "Mistakes happen," he said. "But apologies shouldn't be a reason to wake us in the middle of the night. If a man feels compelled to apologize, he should. I don't see the issue here."

"That's not all," I said. "Ask Clay about what else is bothering him."

"What is Walt getting at, Clay?"

Clay looked from our father, to me. I couldn't read exactly what lay behind his eyes. It may have been regret or anger, distress or resentment, or some combination of all of them. He stood with his mouth open, but no words came out.

"Clay?" our father asked again, the timbre of his voice a half-click higher and more insistent.

Clay shook his head. The corner of his lip rose almost imperceptibly, and a sound came from his throat, part laugh, part snarl. When he spoke, that swirling cloud of emotions I'd seen in his eyes was swept away by an even stronger storm—a tempest of condescension—though I couldn't be certain how much of that gust actually came from Clay and how much I imagined. "Well, I can't rightly apologize to President Johnson or General Westmoreland, now can I?" he said.

"What are you talking about?" Our father was puzzled; the intent of Clay's remark hadn't reached him. In the hallway, though, I could tell that Clay's comment had registered with our mother. She shook her head, and even in the low light, I could see her worry and concern.

"For doing our country wrong," Clay said. "Haven't you been teaching us certain lessons ever since we were big enough to listen? Duty. Honor. Obligation. You answer the call, right?" Clay was becoming more and more animated, punctuating his words with gestures, his eyes growing wide to accentuate the immensity of the point he was trying to make. "I've denied our country of my brother when she needs him most—and I've deprived my brother of an opportunity to do right by the country that gives us our freedom."

Somewhere in his mind, I knew Clay must have been hearing the inspirational score to one of the guts-and-glory Republic Pictures classics that aired on Channel 2's Sunday Matinee, but I saw that our mother heard something entirely different. Outside my door, she sagged beneath an invisible weight. She looked older than I'd ever seen her, and tired.

My father's response surprised me, if simply for the fact that I didn't know how to read it. As Clay spoke, I saw part of him swell with pride at his teaching having taken root with his prized pupil. He thrust his chest and pulled his shoulders back; he probably heard the same soundtrack as Clay. But as Clay delivered his clincher about depriving me of an opportunity, a bit of the air left my father's chest, and his shoulders drooped slightly. The earnest pride on his face became tinged with disgust and what, on any other person, I'd have read as fear; having never seen it on my father, however, I didn't know what to make of it. He clamped his mouth shut and drew a deep breath that made his nostrils flare.

When he exhaled, he seemed, for a heartbeat, bone-tired, but he quickly recovered. "You," he said, pointing at me, "lights out. And you," he said, turning to Clay and stepping close enough to punctuate what he said with a stiff poke of his index finger to my brother's chest, "get to sleep. Those cows won't milk themselves in the morning."

Clay looked down at his chest as if expecting a mark where our father had touched him. "Yes, sir," he said. Clay gave me one last look, a mix of pity and disdain, before walking past our mother toward his room.

My father sighed and stepped through the door to stand next to my mother. With the side of his index finger, he raised her chin and looked into her eyes. His lips moved, but I couldn't hear what he said. She nodded and clenched her jaw before she turned with my father, his arm now encircling her waist, and together they descended the stairs.

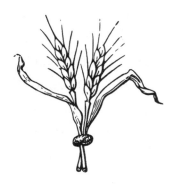

August 22 – 23, 1968

LITTLE WAS SAID about Clay's "apology" in the weeks that followed—my family again showing its German roots. My parents and brother busied themselves with the never-ending chores of operating the farm and preparing for the long winter ahead. I maintained what had become my summer routine since getting out of the hospital—reading, journaling, and best of all, spending time with Meg. I told her about the incident with Clay when she came by the next day. She'd felt the turbulence, observing that my mom was more guarded and reserved—not less kind to her than she'd been, not less willing to interact with her, but Meg sensed that a part of my mom was somewhere else.

The time with Meg ended when she had to pack her bags and head to Madison for Welcome Week prior to the beginning of the year. Her departure was bittersweet. We enjoyed our final, imagined visit to the meadow on a blanket spread beneath the box elder beside the farmhouse. The Oconto County Fair had begun that day in Gillett, and when my parents and Clay had finished the evening chores, they cleaned up to go to the fairgrounds, where they'd visit the livestock buildings, politely "oohing" and "aahing" the brushed cows and soft rabbits, the exotic breeds of chicken, the scrubbed bright pink of the pigs lolling on stark white wood shavings. When Clay and I were younger, we'd then have gone to the midway, where our parents splurged on the wristband for unlimited rides for the two of us, but now, I knew the three of them would go to the exhibit buildings, where my mom would survey the produce and preserves with a critical eye, my dad would inspect the whitetail head mounts displayed by area taxidermists and dream of the coming fall hunt, and Clay would pretend to take it all in when in reality he was hoping to see some cute young thing strolling through, glowing with a summer tan, just as I'd done before Meg arrived almost two years earlier.

As Meg and I sat beneath the box elder, my father and brother got into the old Plymouth, my brother looking in our direction, my father offering a polite wave. My mother briefly swung by our picnic before going to the car. "Keep him out of trouble, Meg," she said. "That cast is coming off soon. Walt might be feeling a bit more wound up than usual."

"I'll always take care of him, Mrs. Neumann," she replied. She turned to me, and I saw that look in her eye. I was ready for my parents to leave.

"I know you will," my mom said then walked to the car.

"I love your mom," Meg said. She poured herself a glass of lemonade and asked if I'd like a refill. I handed her my glass and she filled it, the ice cubes clinking on the side. "To us," she said, raising her glass.

"To us," I said. A slight ping accompanied our glasses touching, and we both drank. I set my glass down and dried my fingers, wet from condensation, on the blanket before placing my hand on Meg's leg. It was warm beneath the flowered cotton print of her skirt. Daisies.

"That's nice," she said. She leaned into me, resting her head on my chest.

I kissed the top of her head. Her hair smelled of lilacs. "What a summer."

"That's putting it lightly," she said. "Listen here, mister. I'm going to miss you these next several months."

"Likewise," I said. Since our first stroll to the meadow in the fall of our Junior year, there'd hardly been a day that we hadn't seen each other. "I envy your being in Madison, too. You won't have to spend the next four-and-a-half months with the stiffest upper lips in all of Gillett."

"No pity parties, though," she said. "Your dad and Clay—that's tough, but you've got your mom. Give her some credit."

"I know," I said. "I've always felt that Mom gets me on another level."

"So talk to her," Meg said.

"Easier said than done." I remembered my father's silent words to her in the hall outside my room, her nodded agreement, their going down the stairs together.

"But here's your chance—no school until January. No Basic or deployment *ever*." Her words floated in the August air. "I still say a 'thank you' every day for that botched double play, whatever Clay might say."

"Me too," I said. "I don't know if—"

Meg cut me off. "But that's no longer an issue." She gave me her devilish look. "You'd have made it. *We'd* have made it. After all," she said, shifting to kneel above me, her knees on either side of my thighs, "the best things are always worth waiting for—like Memorial Day, right?" She flounced her skirt so that it draped over us and wiggled just enough so that I felt her warmth.

"Absolutely," I said, placing my hands low on her back to draw her even closer.

"Good," she said, pulling her hair back to slip it into a pony tail. She was wearing what she called her "moth-to-a-flame" lip gloss. "Since I'm leaving tomorrow," she said, "you should really give me a going-away present." The agate rested on her smooth skin. It had been a warm day, but as the shadows lengthened with the approaching sunset, a cool breeze momentarily came from the west, and I briefly caught the scent of autumn. We both felt the goose bumps rise on our skin before Meg shifted, gliding against me to achieve the desired effect.

"Yes," I said, "I couldn't agree more."

When the phone rang the next morning, I was surprised to hear my mother call me from downstairs. Meg would already have left for Madison with her parents. Since graduation, most of my friends had gone their own ways—some, like Meg, had left for college; others were biding their time, waiting for the draft board to call their numbers; some had even enlisted. When I picked up the receiver and said hello, I was pleasantly surprised to hear Mr. Grzesch on the other end of the line.

"Walter Neumann, it's good to hear you're still alive"

"Hey, Mr. G. I'm surviving, thanks."

"Not up and walking yet?"

"Not yet, but I've become pretty nimble on my crutches."

"Nimble enough to meet up with me for an hour or two— maybe grab a burger at the 4H food stand at the fair?"

The suggestion of the burger made my mouth water. "Let me check with my mom. Still under their roof, still their rules. She's been my doctor's T.J. Eckleberg all summer." I thought of the night before with Meg and gave thanks that even T.J. Eckleberg couldn't see everything. "Can you hold for a second?"

"No problem."

I covered the mouthpiece of the receiver and ran Mr. Grzesch's invitation past my mom as she scrubbed potatoes at the sink.

"First time out since leaving the hospital, Walt—you're feeling up to it?"

"I think I'll manage."

"And you'll be good to your knee?"

"Of course, mom."

"Your teacher knows how to get here?

"Mom…"

"Have fun, Walt."

I put the handset back to my ear. "It's a go, Mr. G."

"Good," he said. "I'll be there in a half-hour?"

"Excellent," I said.

When Mr. Grzesch arrived, my dad and Clay were in the front yard, loading twine into the baler and feeding it through the stringers. Later in the day, they'd bale straw, now sufficiently dry after the oats had been combined two days earlier. I can't say that I missed that job. Baling, be it hay or straw, wasn't pleasant—not snagging bales with a hook and toting and stacking them on the flat rack, not dismantling the interlocking bales on the flat rack to send them on the flights of the elevator climbing into the mow, not snatching the bales off the end of the elevator to re-assemble them in the barn's mow where they'd wait to be used or eaten as the months progressed and the cycle began again the next year. I certainly didn't miss sweating endlessly through my shirt and jeans, the particles of chaff I didn't breathe into my lungs clinging to my damp clothes, transforming me into a human/vegetable hybrid.

I waited on the front porch, champing at the bit to leave home for the first time since returning from the hospital, eager, as I always was, to converse with my teacher. Mr. Grzesch stepped out of his car, a green 1964 Barracuda conspicuous for the sportiness that separated it from most of the other cars around town, and waved to me. I returned a quick wave, positioned myself between my crutches, and descended the stairs. "Hey, Mr. Grzesch," I said. It felt somewhat odd, as though seeing such a significant figure from one part of my life here at my home tilted the universe out of balance. Holing up in my bedroom with books and notebooks was one thing, but seeing Mr. Grzesch standing in the driveway between my house and the barn was something else entirely.

"Hey, Walt," he said as he stepped toward me. "You seem to be getting along okay on those things." He nodded toward my crutches.

"I manage," I said. "My room's upstairs, but the dinner table and bathroom are down. As much as my mom loves me, she doesn't serve breakfast in bed or do bedpan duty."

"Gotcha," Mr. Grzesch said. He clapped me on the shoulder. Seeing my father and Clay at the baler—and being curious by nature—Mr. Grzesch nodded in their direction. "What are your dad and brother doing?" he asked.

"Loading the baler with twine. They'll be baling straw today."

"Miss it?" he asked.

"I miss walking a lot," I said, "but baling? Not so much."

"That bad?"

"It's not the greatest."

Mr. Grzesch chuckled. "Mind if I say hello and check it out?" he asked.

"Be my guest," I said, gesturing with one of the crutches. We made our way toward my father and Clay, Mr. Grzesch ambling, me swinging with an odd syncopation.

"Hello, Mr. Neumann," Mr. Grzesch said. "Clay."

My father paused, twine in hand trailing from one of the threaders. "Good morning, Mr. Grzesch," he said. Clay offered a curt nod.

"Walter tells me you're baling straw this afternoon?"

"The straw's dry and the weather's right. We need to get it done before Clay starts school next week."

Mr. Grzesch looked at me and then back to my father. "If

Walt worked half as hard for you as he did in my classes, you're down more than a little in the manual labor department, Mr. Neumann."

"My boys know the meaning of a day's work," my father said, "but if something like Walt's injury comes up, we all just pick each other up and make things go." His tone of voice was matter-of-fact, but on a lower register I detected something else.

"But an extra hand wouldn't hurt?" asked Mr. Grzesch.

"Only a fool turns down help," my father said.

"Trust an English teacher?" asked Mr. Grzesch.

My father looked over Mr. Grzesch. I couldn't imagine he approved of the soft, frayed jeans or the worn leather sandals that left most of Mr. Grzesch's feet exposed, but if he disapproved, he didn't show it. "A strong arm depends upon a stronger will," he said.

"What time will you begin today?" asked Mr. Grzesch.

"Dew's still drying. We'll start after lunch. Around one o'clock."

"I'm in," said Mr. Grzesch, grinning.

"It's much appreciated," my father said.

I was confused. Part of me felt more than a little proud of Mr. Grzesch. My injury, in addition to the gift it had delivered me, had also presented my family with challenges that summer, a circumstance about which I did feel a degree of guilt when I saw my parents and brother bone-tired at the end of the day. But what I knew of Mr. Grzesch's background—that he'd grown up on the south side of Chicago, that he'd gone against neighborhood allegiances to root for the north side Cubs, that he'd never known his father (who'd died while Mr. Grzesch was an infant), that he'd attended DePaul University—hadn't exactly prepared him to bale straw.

"It will be my pleasure," Mr. Grzesch said. He turned to my brother. "Looking forward to senior year, Clay?"

"Looking forward to it being over," he said. Clay had had Mr. Grzesch for English as a junior, and as was characteristic of every subject for my brother, had performed in as average a fashion as possible.

"Why's that?" Mr. Grzesch asked. I winced. I wasn't sure if Mr. Grzesch knew what door he was opening. "I've heard around town that more than a few scouts like the way you play shortstop. They were easy to spot at games, scribbling in their notebooks."

My father looked from Mr. Grzesch to Clay. Clay looked at me—a strange day was becoming even stranger—then back to Mr. Grzesch. "Those scouts will have to wait a few years, Mr. Grzesch. My country needs me, and I plan to enlist in the United States Army on my eighteenth birthday. I will go to Basic Training shortly after graduating next spring, and after that, I'll become a Screaming Eagle."

I could see my father's pride increase with each word from Clay's lips, and I felt myself cringe. Had I said anything resembling that to Mr. Grzesch, I'd have expected him to either faint in disbelief or start searching for a hidden camera from *Candid Camera*. But when I heard Clay say aloud for the first time what everyone in our family knew in our hearts, Mr. Grzesch was nonplussed. "You sound very certain about that, Clay, and our nation is truly blessed by the service of young men as dedicated as you."

But while Mr. Grzesch may not have skipped a beat in responding to Clay, my heart skipped several. The man who'd talked me through the particulars of fleeing to Canada should I have chosen that option—and had even praised those brazen enough to burn their draft cards—seemed to have adopted the mindset of my father, the point of view that had more than once nearly brought my father and me to fisticuffs. My universe had turned in an instant, and when Mr. Grzesch motioned toward his car, I paused to gather myself. Seeing the look on my face, Mr. Grzesch arched an eyebrow; he mouthed *it's okay* to me and looked at his watch. "I promised Walt lunch at the fair, Mr. Neumann, so we're going to grab a bite to eat. I'll be back by one o'clock."

"One o'clock," my father said.

Mr. Grzesch took my crutches and placed them in the back seat of his car as I slid into the passenger seat. Getting into my teacher's vehicle was strange enough, but given everything that had just transpired, I couldn't speak.

"Weirded out, Walt?" asked Mr. Grzesch. He shifted gears as we drove up the dead end road named after my family once my grandparents had settled there and built the farm after coming from Germany.

"That's putting it mildly, Mr. G. You don't even know."

The light filtering through the hardwoods lining either side of the lane cast my teacher in a shifting quilt of light and dark. He looked at me, inhaled and opened his mouth as if to speak, but nothing came out. We continued driving in silence to Gillett, a drive that felt much longer than its five minutes. Mr. Grzesch pulled into the fairgrounds and handed a quarter to the attendant.

He parked beneath a tree near the beer garden and food stands tucked behind the grandstand where the annual horse pull was taking place. To our right, the steel and neon framework of the carnival rides rose from the hard-packed earth, not yet awakened by the shouts and anticipation of children eager to be spun and twirled until they were numbed by centrifugal force and the sugary haze of cotton candy and snow cones. A few of the carnies milled about the midway, the tents of their rigged carnival games still shuttered as they pulled at cigarettes.

"Let's head over to the 4-H stand and have a talk." Mr. Grzesch opened his door, pulled my crutches from the back seat of his Barracuda, and made his way to my side of the car.

I boosted myself out of the seat, standing on my good leg, and took my crutches from him. "Thanks," I said, positioning the pads beneath my arms to swing away from the car.

"Did I ever tell you the first meal I ate in Gillett was at the 4-H stand during the fair?" Mr. Grzesch asked.

"No," I said.

"Yeah," he said. "I'd come up here for my second interview, after which Mr. Eiseth offered me the job. I immediately accepted, and I felt like celebrating. I'd seen the hubbub going on here as I drove into town, so I decided to check things out.

"The interview had been later in the day—Mr. Eiseth knew I was driving up from Chicago—and the fairgrounds had come to life." We made our way from our parking spot to the cluster of food stands. Mr. Grzesch stopped and extended his arms, made a sweeping gesture all around us. "I was feeling a buzz. My first job out of college, and now the lights, the rides, the sound of the machines, the barkers calling from the games, preying on the machismo of guys out to impress the girls and parents who can't say no to their kids. Growing up in Chicago, I'd never seen anything like a county fair." He shook his head. "Wrigleyville could get a little crazy on game days, of course, and I loved that." Though Mr. Grzesch was only seven years older than me, he looked even younger when he mentioned Wrigleyville, like a boy whose dream had come true. "The Miracle Mile always has an undertow of life, and the ethnic neighborhoods back home each have their own flavor. When I was a kid, Navy Pier had acts and attractions that came through. But this," he said, looking around us, "this county fair was so different. It was like Twain, dear Uncle Walt, and Ginsberg had conspired to build a temporary city fueled by dreams and urges, hopes and wishes. The barns were filled with animals scrubbed and brushed and hosed down until they gleamed. The exhibition halls were lined with shelves of home-canned preserves glowing within their Mason jars. Children carried balloons in one hand and pink and blue cotton candy on a stick in the other. Young people like you moved in clusters, boys eyeing girls who giggled at knowing they were firmly in their sights, transcending the tedium in which they'd come to know each other in school." As he spoke, Mr. Grzesch had taken on the look he did when he delivered his best lectures, lost somewhere in the ether of ideas he sought to bring to life through the truths they possessed and the very force of his will.

And as Mr. Grzesch again became the teacher whose vision had changed me, the feelings verging on betrayal and disbelief just a half-hour earlier evaporated. I'd gone to the Oconto County

Youth Fair ever since I could remember. I'd ridden the rides and played the games. I'd surveyed the barns and exhibition halls and stood in the clusters of boys awkwardly situated between youth and manhood. And I'd sensed on a lower level the very things that Mr. Grzesch now conjured to life, but I'd never been able to articulate them—and I was freshly reminded of what Mr. Grzesch had done for me over the last two years, of how he'd given me a new pair of glasses through which I might view the world, of what I wanted to do with my life, of how the leg whose cast would soon be removed had made possible the promises this man had helped me envision. "Amazing, Mr. G," I said.

"You give me too much credit, Walt," he said. "I'm only doing what comes naturally to me—and comes to you, too. I just happen to have a few years on you." We sat on one of the backless benches at the 4-H food stand, I at the end so I could prop my leg up on the bench at the counter perpendicular to ours. "A few years from now with a college degree in your back pocket, you'll make my riff on county fairs look like child's play." He winked at me. "Besides," he said, "the true measure of a teacher is that the student no longer needs him—the student is ready to move on, take the next step. I feel like you've absorbed everything I have to offer you and then some. I'm just a step on what I hope proves a rather remarkable journey for you." He motioned to one of the 4-H members working the stand, an earnest-looking boy of 8 or 9 who wore thick-rimmed glasses and held a pad of order tickets in one hand and clutched a chisel-tipped Dixon Ticonderoga in the other.

Mr. Grzesch made sense, but I wasn't ready to completely

embrace his model of the student no longer needing his teacher; to do so would have felt like betraying him, and I wasn't in the habit of doing that to anyone, least of all Mr. Grzesch. We placed our orders, and soon the same boy who'd taken our orders brought us our food. Each of us had a cheeseburger with fried onions, an order of crinkle-cut French fries delivered piping hot in a paper cup with golden yellow fries printed against a burnt orange background, and a Sun Drop with tiny citrus flakes dancing in the carbonation. "The little man working the stand looks like a mini-Walt," Mr. Grzesch said.

I laughed. "He's got the serious look," I said, "but he looks more like a catcher than a second baseman to me."

Mr. Grzesch took a bite of his burger. "God, that's good," he said. "The first burger I had after being offered my job was fantastic, but I thought maybe I was just riding the high of scoring the first paying job to ever demand more of my mind than my body—so I ordered another, and it was just as good."

"That burger you're eating may have been grazing on Neumann pasture land not too long ago," I said. "Every year, when we butcher in the spring, my parents donate a side of beef to the 4-H that gets ground into the hamburger they serve at this stand for the fair."

"Had I known the meat from your farm was this good, I'd have angled for an invitation to your house for dinner a long time ago," he said.

"It is good," I said, "and my mom knows her way around a kitchen." I pictured her pulling a sheet of cookies from the oven. "When I was a kid, my birthday was the one all the other kids in class looked forward to because they knew my mom would send something homemade and delicious—chocolate chip cookies with bits of butternut from the tree in our yard, or her chocolate cupcakes with cream cheese and chocolate chips in the middle."

"Does labor get paid in food at the Neumann's?" Mr. Grzesch asked.

"I couldn't see it going any other way. If there's one thing my mom does, it's feed people. You should have seen her with Meg this summer," I said. "She tried passing on a lifetime of garden and kitchen knowledge in a month-and-a-half."

Mr. Grzesch smiled. "That's a good sign," he said. "I paired you with Meg for peer review that first time because you were the two best students in my class, but I wasn't surprised that you hit it off so well. It's good seeing you two together, and it's good to hear that your mom has taken to her, too."

"She has," I said, picturing the two of them pressing raspberry pulp through a conical sieve as they made jam. "My parents surprise me sometimes," I said sipping Sun Drop through a straw.

"How's that?" Mr. Grzesch asked.

"They're only a generation removed from their German roots and tend to be rather insular. They don't typically bring in outsiders to do or even help with any kind of work on the farm. They're usually too stubborn to realize they could use help, and even less likely to ask if they acknowledged it. I wasn't too surprised, though, that they allowed Meg to visit me as much as she did. They knew, especially my mom, that Meg was the best antidote for me, but I was surprised when she and my mom did as much as they did together. I was even more surprised that my father took you up on your offer to help today," I said. "Speaking of which—"

"I know," Mr. Grzesch said, "I owe you an explanation."

"Not because you asked to help with the straw," I said. "That was great of you, and as much as my parents would never let us be perceived as unable to take care of things on our own, I know that come the end of the day, they'll be grateful to have your help."

"I'm a city boy, but I believe that 'an honest day's work' applies to farm labor more than exercising the brain. That's something I've picked up from you over the last two years. I doubt you'll ever take over your parents' farm, but I don't think anyone or anything will ever be able to take that farm out of you. It's one of the things that's going to make you atypical when you dive into the English department in Madison. They may have other students who'll vie with you for the top spot in the pecking order, but the thing that will always give you an edge is your knowledge of work, of how to stick with something and see it through. That has to come from your upbringing on the farm. It's fundamental to your makeup." Mr. Grzesch placed several fries in his mouth. "Reminds me of working summers in the Gary Steel Works through college."

I was both surprised and buoyed. Surprised because he didn't often mention working in a steel mill. I'd read about Carnegie's steel mills, the fire, the heat, the danger, and though Mr. Grzesch would have been working in the mill in the early to mid-Sixties, I couldn't imagine that the fire, heat, and danger would have been much less for him than it had been for the earliest mill workers.

I was buoyed because he'd again made me feel that I had something special to offer the world—and because he'd again seen a something in me that showed he cared about me beyond my ability to discuss books and compose sentences artfully. "I want to hear about you in the mills some time, but you still need to explain what you said to Clay."

"Right," he said.

"I mean, I know, or thought I'd known, your feelings about what's going on over there, and I thought we were on the same page—"

"You do, Walt," he said, cutting me off. "We are. Pardon my French, but it's a fucked-up war being fought for all the wrong reasons."

"So where does that 'blessed by the dedicated service' business come from?"

"I meant what I said to your brother." He set down the last of his cheeseburger on the waxy paper on the counter in front of him. "Look, Clay isn't the one who started that turkey shoot, no more than anyone else being shipped over there instigated it. It's politicians, generals, defense contractors—they're the ones making this thing go. They paint it as black and white, 'us v. them,' 'democracy v. communism.'"

"*We* know that—but isn't volunteering like Clay plans to do an iron-clad guarantee that those people will keep making war and painting those pictures?"

"That's the elephant in the room," Mr. Grzesch said. And for the next several minutes, despite their deliciousness, our cheeseburgers grew cold on the counter as Mr. Grzesch and I discussed the ideal America and the importance of defending such an experiment; discussed whether service, be it willing or compulsory, simply fueled a fire tended by decision-makers drunk on power and profits; discussed the treatment of the young vets returning from Vietnam, especially since news of My Lai had broken almost six months earlier, and how terms like "baby killer" and "it's too bad you didn't die over there" had entered the American vernacular; and discussed the unfortunate fact that soldiers couldn't select the conflict in which they fought. We both agreed that we'd have volunteered for World War II, when demarcations between right and wrong felt far more definite than the shifting lines in the sand being drawn and re-drawn at our moment.

But for as indefinite and unfortunate as those circumstances were—for as devastatingly as they altered the lives of soldiers, their families, friends, and lovers, and an entire nation—the point from which Mr. Grzesch would not sway was his belief that once a young man was all-in, whether he'd volunteered or had been drafted, the task he performed for the nation and its people warranted the utmost respect and dignity. "Fight the politicians who concoct these travesties, and stay out of it by whatever means possible if it doesn't align with your heart and soul. That's why I hashed all that out with you, Walt, and would have stood behind you if the golden ticket hadn't come your way. If you'd been compelled to opt for more extreme measures to stay out of it—hey, Thoreau's time in the hoosegow prompted *Civil Disobedience,* right?—I'd have been at the front of the line to help you, but when a young man is in, he's in, and on some level, he's fighting for you and me and every one of us."

Mr. Grzesch's words flipped a switch in my head. I looked at the people around us, the same people who lined the parade route and the memorial plot three months earlier, who lined the pews at my church and walked the halls of my high school, who bellied up and bent elbows at the bars that outnumbered other businesses in my hometown—and as I looked at them, I didn't see them in an entirely new light, but in a light that had a different character, one that allowed me to recognize features I'd somehow never before noticed. And I didn't know yet just what those features meant—just that they were there and new, something I'd need to think about. I looked at Mr. Grzesch as he finished his cheeseburger and thought of standing in the back row of the marching band at the memorial marker as Meg played "Taps." I thought of the new names on the marker and how I'd feared mine being added to the list. The names. I'd known the young men whose names had been added that day. I'd always looked at those lives lost as a waste. I'd viewed those who fought in wars, and especially Vietnam, as either unfortunate victims or hoodwinked pawns in an insidious game beyond their comprehension, and while those sentiments didn't disappear in the hot August air, I felt something new blossoming for the first time, something that took root and sent fragile tendrils skyward. Something that felt like understanding.

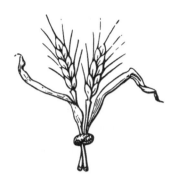

September 3, 1968

NOT BEING IN a classroom when September began felt surreal. I watched Clay climb onto the bus taking him to the school where I'd spent the lion's share of the last thirteen years of my life, knowing I wouldn't glide past the trophy case on my way to my locker just outside the cafeteria, wouldn't take a seat in the just-finished gymnasium for Mr. Lindow's oh-so-thrilling beginning of the year assembly, wouldn't be hanging out in Mr. Grzesch's room at every opportunity with Meg. I wouldn't start classes in Madison until mid-January.

Even more surreal was Meg not being there. She'd already sent a postcard from Madison—a shot of the State Capitol lit up at night atop the high point of the isthmus on which the city was built—and I was pleased to hear that orientation had gone well, that she was getting along swimmingly with her roommate (a fellow art major named Audrey from a small town just outside Green Bay), that her classes were leaving her a bit nervous but hopeful, and best of all, that she couldn't wait for me to join her in Madison spring semester.

After the bus rolled up Neumann Lane, I sat alone at the kitchen table, vestiges of corn flakes growing soggy as my parents finished morning chores. They'd already been up since 5 am. My mother had imposed a family policy that on school days, Clay and I wouldn't have to get up to milk before going to school. My father, who believed one of the necessities of having children on a farm was to squeeze whatever labor was possible from them, deferred to my mother on this one, and on her insistence that Clay and I be able to participate in extra-curriculars after school hours.

I ate the last of the corn flakes, drank the last of the milk from the bowl, and looked around me. No school, no Meg, no Mr. Grzesch. The day's silver lining, I hoped, would be my appointment at the clinic in Shawano. Dr. Burgess, pleased by the progress he had seen in my x-rays during my previous appointment, had decided my cast could come off for good and I could begin rehabilitation. One day shy of two months, and I was excited to begin walking again, even if they were baby steps.

I'd just begun writing a letter to Meg when my mother came in to clean up before our trip to Shawano. "It's a big day, Walter."

I patted the cast. "I won't miss this thing," I said. "Just about everything has been a challenge." I twirled the pen between my thumb and index finger. "But at the same time, I'd be lying if I said it wasn't worth it."

"I know," my mother said. She patted my shoulder. "I know. More than one person's prayers were answered that day."

"Thanks, Mom," I said. I'd long felt that my mother understood me in a way my father didn't, wouldn't, or maybe even couldn't. Whereas he was the stern taskmaster whose solution to any problem was attacking it with hard work that more than compensated for any shortcomings in planning or strategy, my mother was caring and nurturing. She was no less a hard worker than my father—and she was no less dedicated to her principles than he was—but she also had a softness that aligned with my vision of the world.

"Did you have enough for breakfast?" she asked. "I can get you something more if you like."

"No thanks," I said. "I'm good." I also knew that when we were done at the clinic, she would stop at the L & L Ranch, a truck stop on the eastern edge of Shawano, to treat me to lunch. That was my mother—if she could sneak a little something special to Clay or me, or find a reason to celebrate, she did. McDonald's stops on our rare trips into Green Bay, a dollar bill slipped discreetly into my coat pocket for a hot dog and a soda at a basketball or baseball game, the chocolate chip cookies tucked into my backpack when I opened it at my locker in the morning.

I continued my letter as my mother readied herself. I wondered just what Meg was doing at that moment. Which class would she be in? How different was it from high school? Was she wearing her pendant? We both knew that school would demand more of her time and attention than it had previously, and that we wouldn't be able to use Mr. Grzesch's class as an excuse for the "study sessions" we both enjoyed, but we'd make it. Before my injury, we'd resolved to make it through two years, so we could certainly tolerate a few months. Besides, there was a fall break and the Thanksgiving holiday, and the Eiseths had promised to take me to Madison when they went to visit Meg. I finished the letter and placed it in an envelope, addressed and stamped it, and made what I hoped would be my last trip to the mailbox on crutches.

On my way back to the house, I swung by the machine shed, where my father was preparing equipment to begin chopping corn and putting up silage. He stood at the grindstone, and I watched from a safe distance as he sharpened the triangular knives mounted on an eight-foot bar that would slice through the dense stalks of corn, allowing them to be chewed up by the powerful chopper and blown through a chute into the chopper box pulled behind it. He wore protective glasses and handled the knife-lined bar with hands clad in scarred gloves, their leather old and dense and impervious to even the knives so long as the person handling them was wise. And my father was. He turned and grasped the bar so that he brought knife to grindstone precisely, steel and stone meeting, sending out quick showers of orange sparks that burst and danced on the concrete floor before disappearing.

When he finished sharpening the last knife, he placed the bar on his workbench, turned off the electric motor that spun the grindstone, and faced me. "Are you ready for that to come off, Walt?" he asked, nodding at my cast.

"More than I can say," I said.

He paused a moment, as though measuring his response. "I'm happy for you," he said.

"Thanks," I said. "I don't know that I'm going to be able to milk cows anytime soon—"

"No, that's not it," he said. "Though it would be nice to have a full crew back at work, we'll make do. Besides, you were supposed to have been gone anyway. Everyone just totes a bit more of the load."

I didn't know how to take his response. *Supposed to have been gone anyway.* I couldn't read what lay behind his words, and I didn't want to risk an argument. "That was nice, though, of Mr. Grzesch to help out with baling straw the other day, no?"

My father removed the protective glasses. "It was," he said. "Your teacher—he's a good man."

My father's response surprised me. For too long, he'd put it in not-so-subtle terms that he believed my position on Vietnam and the potential of military service, be it compulsory or voluntary, came more from Mr. Grzesch than it did from my having thought things through for myself or standing by principles he mistook for someone else's. "I know," I said. "Best teacher I've ever had, and he's never shown himself as anything but equal to that as a person."

"He showed me something," my father said. Visible acts, black-and-white deeds, were the foundation of my father's perspective on life. Elbow grease, perspiration, and sore joints at the end of the day meant something to my father. I remembered watching from the front porch as Mr. Grzesch, decked out in the old jeans, denim shirt, and work boots he'd retrieved from his apartment, took my place in the ebb and flow of work that day. After a short course in the operation of the old John Deere my father called "Poopy John," Mr. Grzesch began driving empty flat racks out to the field where my father and Clay had begun baling, and fell into the rotation as they alternated between pulling the baler and flat rack with our International-Harvester tractor, stacking the flat rack high with interlocking bales of straw, and returning home with a wagon full of golden bales. Once all three racks had been filled, they were pulled up to the screeching old elevator angled into the upstairs mow of the barn. Two men went into the mow—one to toss bales from the elevator to the other, who stacked them in the same interlocking pattern used on the racks in the field—and the third remained outside, first to engage the power take-off arm of the elevator to the PTO gear on Poopy John and send the elevator flights climbing, then to disassemble the bales from the rack and place them on the elevator. I couldn't see Mr. Grzesch at work in the mow, but seeing him on the wagon, I could tell he wasn't a stranger to manual labor. His work shirt was dark with sweat. The dust and chaff of the bales clung to him, but he never missed a beat, keeping the bales moving on the elevator three at a time, equally spaced, just the way my father liked it. Between loads, he and my father and brother would take long pulls of ice water from the thermal jugs my mother had prepared for each of them, and I could only imagine that it was as welcome and refreshing to Mr. Grzesch as it had always been to me.

"I'm glad he showed you something," I said. My father and I had found ample opportunity to disagree with each other over the last two years, so I was comforted to know that we were capable of seeing eye-to-eye on something.

"I shouldn't be surprised, though—what with his father having fought in World War II. Sad that he lost his life over in Europe, but it sounds like his mother did a fine job of bringing him up as his father would have wanted. Plus, summers in a steel mill. That must have really been something. Your teacher," he said, "knows what's important. It's in his blood."

The cache with my father given the fate of Mr. Grzesch's father didn't surprise me. Mr. Grzesch had told me the story of his parents coming to America from Poland, about never knowing his father, who'd left his job at the Gary Works to volunteer for his adopted homeland and die on the beaches of Normandy, and about how his mother Stella ("for star," as he always said whenever he mentioned her name) raised him and his sister on the south side of Chicago. I was somewhat surprised, though, to hear that my father knew about Mr. Grzesch working at a steel mill, something I hadn't known about beyond his having done it. But when my father mentioned it, he shook his head in a way that made me suspect he knew something I didn't.

I was envious, but I wasn't going to press my luck. "He knows," I agreed, confident that I spoke the truth even though my father and I may have been addressing two entirely different things.

My mother was noticeably more upbeat as we sat across the table from each other at the L&L Ranch. Things had gone well at the doctor's office—the cast had come off without complication, and my leg, though the skin had taken on a ghostly pallor, hadn't withered away to nothing. My first steps, though tentative, didn't send me sprawling onto the floor of the examination room, and Dr. Burgess laid out a rehabilitation program for me that emphasized strengthening the muscles in my injured leg as a way of protecting the joint. He cautioned against overdoing things.

My mother set her menu down on the table. "Whatever you want. Another in what I know will be a long line of celebrations for you, Walt."

"I hope so, Mom." I placed my hand near my knee and felt my leg. The skin was sensitive, but actually feeling the denim of my jeans and the warmth of my hand was so refreshingly different compared to the sensation of being encased in plaster that I didn't mind the tiny pinpricks of pain dancing along the surface of my skin.

"Of course it is!" she said. "Now my only worry will be that your professors don't work you too hard." The image of Clay boarding the bus that morning crossed my mind. What my mother didn't say hung in the air between us, but I trusted a solution would be found once both Clay and I had left home. "But even that's not so bad," she quickly added. "You've always done well in school, and Meg will be down there with you. You two will look after one another."

"Thanks, Mom," I said. "You made quite an impression on her this summer."

"She made one on me, too," she said. The ice in her water clinked against the glass as she raised it to take a drink. "You and Clay and your father are the greatest blessings in my life," she said, "but I wouldn't have minded having a daughter, too." She silently placed her glass in the same spot from which she'd taken it, aligning the base with the sweat ring it had left on the table. "It's nice having another member of the fairer sex around." She sighed and folded her hands on top of her menu.

"Sharing that recipe with you was a big deal," I said.

"I know," my mother said, still looking down but with a smile tugging at the corners of her mouth. "It's only shared with exclusive company."

I hadn't known that Meg shared the Eiseth's unwritten rule about family recipes with my mother. It had always been a given that Meg and I were close and that my parents felt she was as good for me as the Eiseths felt I was good for her, but I'd never had *that* conversation with either of my parents. I didn't know what to say.

My mother patted my hand. "If that's what God has in the cards *someday*," she said, "your father and I certainly won't have any complaints. Just don't be in a hurry," she said. "You're different in so many ways from anyone on either side of the family— and different isn't bad. Different can be good. In your case, it's a very good thing. Appreciate and put to use the many gifts you've been given. Count your blessings. Enjoy life. You and Meg will be there for each other. She's a good girl, Walt. A very good girl."

Typically in our family, anything but anger was left unsaid—not because we didn't feel or think deeply, but because it wasn't part of our make-up. My grandparents on both sides of the family had come to America from Germany, and in addition to the language and whatever possessions they could pack into steamer trunks for the journey across the Atlantic, they brought with them stoic temperaments that locked away expressions of genuine fondness to the very people for whom they felt that fondness. My father was the textbook example; he could boast about Clay and me to anyone—and he often did—but when the opportunity was there for him to express pride or love directly to us, the words remained locked inside. It was assumed that we would see his love in his actions, namely, his unending work to make our farm successful and provide for our family. While my grandmother had shown me glimpses of the kind of warmth I loved, it was my mother who had started chipping away at that old country mindset the most, and she'd passed that trait along to me. Throughout much of my youth, I had felt precariously balanced between the desire to express my feelings and the necessity of keeping them under wraps.

"Thanks, Mom," I said. I felt that I'd been offering her thanks more often than usual in recent weeks. I'd always felt that beneath her silence in my conflicts with my father, she understood things—not that she necessarily understood my reasoning, but that she understood the language of the heart and the powerful sway it had on me. Feeling that she understood me on some essential level helped me make it through some very tough times. It gave me confidence and strength. Between her, Meg, and Mr. Grzesch, I had the foundation to stand tall in a world where traditional rules of decency and goodness seemed to have disappeared, leaving the America I imagined precariously perched between grandeur and ruin.

The waitress took our orders: my mother, the spaghetti and meat sauce she said almost made her wish she were Italian, I, the steak and eggs that were part of the breakfast menu available 24/7. "Red meat to build your strength?" she asked.

"It'll help," I said. "They make a mean sirloin here—just not quite as tasty as yours." I could tell from the way she glanced toward the counter that she appreciated the compliment. "Speaking of which," I said, "during lunch at the fair, Mr. Grzesch couldn't stop praising the burgers at the 4-H stand, and I told him that he was eating meat you and Dad had donated."

Mom smiled. "He did tell me more than once that those burgers at the stand were like 'magic pucks of deliciousness,' whatever that means."

I laughed. "That's Mr. Grzesch for you," I said. "His love of language means you end up hearing him say things you don't hear every day."

My mother gave me a knowing look. "Not that you've ever been told something similar?"

"I'll take that as a compliment, Mom. Besides, his message did seem to get across." When Mr. Grzesch left that night, the last load of straw tightly stacked in the mow, he said his final good-byes to my family while cradling a brown grocery sack packed with packages of hamburger frozen and wrapped in butcher paper and labeled in black marker in my mother's rounded script. "If you were to pay him in hamburger for help, I don't know that he'd give up teaching, but I bet you'd be seeing much more of him."

"It was the least we could do," my mother said. "Your father and Clay could have gotten by. I could have worked on the wagons to get the bales on the elevator. But it would have taken us another day to finish the job."

"Why did Dad accept Mr. Grzesch's offer of help?" I asked. The waitress came to our table balancing a large round serving tray just above her shoulder. She deftly brought it down, balanced on her palm and stabilized by her fingertips, and placed our orders in front of us. "I mean, people have offered help before, but it's like he was too proud to accept such an offer."

She sighed. "I know you've built up an image of your father over the years," she said. She paused, twirling her spaghetti onto her fork. "He's not always an easy man." She placed the forkful of spaghetti into her mouth and chewed slowly. I could tell she was thinking, choosing her words carefully. "And I can understand your seeing him as you do." She dabbed a spot of sauce from her lip with her napkin, then placed it back on her lap. "In some ways, you can be as stubborn as him," she said. "And stubbornness is a strength, in both your cases. So is pride. And hard work. And love," she said. "I know he doesn't show it to you in the way you'd like," she said, "but he does love you and wants what's best for you."

"I've never doubted that he loves me," I said, cutting a piece of steak, the serrated edge of the knife slicing through meat, "it's just that what he thinks is best for me doesn't line up so well with my thoughts on the subject."

"I know," she said. "I know."

"So is he okay now with me going to school in January? He's never said. That's all I ever wanted, Mom—to go to school. I want to carry a backpack full of books across a campus, not the alternative."

"He's...coming to terms with it," she said.

"That's not exactly a ringing endorsement," I said.

"Of course it isn't," she said. "When I was pregnant with you, your father and I knew we were going to have a son. It was just one of those things—we felt it. And from the moment we knew, he started sketching out your future. You were going to be the son who hunted and fished with him, the son who'd learn what he could share about farming and one day take over the farm from us. He saw that as his gift to you, a lifetime's effort at making something you could use to support a family of your own."

"And the army?"

"Yes the army, too," she said. "To him, that's how a young man can and should give back to his country."

"He can't envision any other way? Why not being a teacher and helping people learn and grow? Or writing things that make people think and feel?"

"I know, I know," she said. "I'm with you on that point, Walt." She hesitated. "But I'm with your father as well." She frowned, further accentuating the lines that had already begun creasing her face. "It's possible, you know, that you can both be right."

Hearing it from her reminded me of what Mr. Grzesch had said to Clay and our conversation at the fair, but her words also had a different character. I could feel her love for my father there in the air between us, alive and visceral, but not without scars, not without evidence of her having carried burdens of her own.

"I know," I said grudgingly, knowing that she was right even though I wasn't feeling it, though I did sense her words finding accord with that something I'd first felt at the fair.

"I just wish," she said, again speaking in measured tones, as though reluctant to even bring to the light of day what she was about to say, but she never completed the thought. "I think I understand why your father feels the way he does," she said, "but I don't know just where—"

I didn't let her finish. "He fought the good war, Mom—it was easy for him to paint things black-and-white, especially the way Grandma and Grandpa felt coming here from Germany." I remembered having shared my essay with Meg—of walks and *herrlichkeits* and big ideas that readily lent themselves to broad but powerful generalizations—but I also remembered sharing beech nuts, holding hands, and kissing for the first time in the meadow that autumn afternoon. "I just think Dad has difficulty understanding that while principles may not change, circumstances do. That can make a difference."

"That's true," she said. "And I wish I had more to share with you, Walt. I know the stories you hear aren't terribly detailed. Maybe that's for the best, though. I wish I had more to share." She picked up her utensils and began twirling another forkful of spaghetti. "I wish I knew."

I'd never heard her share such a sentiment, and it struck a chord with me. Over the course of all of our back-and-forth, I'd asked my father, more than once, to tell me about his experiences in World War II, wishing he would share something, anything, that would have made the prospect of Vietnam easier to digest, would give me some glimpse into the life of a soldier and expose me to hard truths that were the source of his perspective. Posing the question made him uncomfortable, and when I was bold enough to press the issue, he angered quickly, his face growing red. His voice sputtered and veins protruded from his temples. When he regained a semblance of composure, he gave me the same platitudes about democracy and service I'd heard a thousand times before he left the room. "Me too," I said. "I've tried."

"So did I," she said. "Before you were born, I tried everything, tried to sneak it into conversations, to ask him over meals, at bedtime, while we worked. Sometimes I was subtle. Other times I was rather forward." She dabbed at the red sauce on her plate with a piece of garlic bread then took a bite and chewed as though picturing something she hadn't seen in some time.

"How did that work for you?" I asked.

She shook her head. "He withdrew. And when I pressed, he fell back on the same line: 'there are things a soldier can't bring home, things he can't share, so he buries them and moves on.'" She paused, as though she wanted to say something more and was thinking of how to phrase it, but she remained silent.

I felt for my mother. Though she was approaching fifty and I'd seen the indicators, I'd never felt she was old until that day, when she spoke of my father not sharing his wartime experiences. The streaks of gray in her dark brown hair were more pronounced, and the lines from the corners of her eyes were markers of age more than the smile lines etched by her easy laughter.

"I'm sorry, Mom," I said, not knowing exactly why I was apologizing. For my father? For circumstance? For something bigger than either of us?

She sighed. "So am I," she said. "Your father has been nothing but good to me and our family, and maybe he's right. Maybe some things can't be shared. Who am I to say? Besides," she said, "you ought to know those stubborn German men." She attempted to smile.

The tone of her voice didn't match the sentiment of her words, though, and I wondered what she wasn't telling me. "He's a good father and a good husband," I said, and while I believed my words, it was belief borne more of my head than my heart. I wondered if he could have been a better father and husband. I thought of Clay and his path and wondered if he'd come back as some version of our father, repeating his lines. I wondered just what could compel me to withhold things from Meg and thanked God Vietnam wouldn't put me in such a circumstance.

My mother and I finished the rest of our meal in silence.

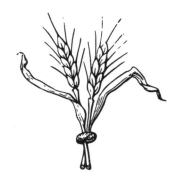

October 12, 1968

LUNCH WITH MY mother had piqued my curiosity about my father's military service, and my weekly meetings with Mr. Grzesch only fueled the fire. We had lunch together each Saturday that fall at OJ's Midtown—an opportunity for us to confer as we had while he was still my teacher and for us to get to know each other even better. I'd already known that his father died in World War II, but on a particular Saturday in mid-October, I also learned of the Silver Star his father had been posthumously awarded for valor on the beaches of Normandy—of how he'd stormed a German machine gun nest, ensuring that no more Allied soldiers would be taken down from that position, before later losing his own life in the countryside of France. "Wouldn't you know it," Mr. Grzesch said, "my father survives

D-Day only to buy the farm at the hands of a German sniper while he's taking a pee. Zapped while zipping. The universe has a strange sense of humor sometimes."

"Do you remember him at all?" I asked.

"I don't," he said. "I was only a year-and-a-half when he enlisted, only two when he died." When he spoke of his father, Mr. Grzesch didn't sound noticeably different. "I have some old photos," he said. "My mom had a family portrait taken shortly before he enlisted. Classic old-world look, sepia tones and everything. My dad's collar is starched and his shirt buttoned all the way to the top button, my mom's in a dark dress with a white lace collar, both of them staring back sternly at the camera as I sit on my father's knee, looking at something off to one side."

"Do you ever regret not knowing him, not having memories?" I asked.

"Not having a father is the one thing I've always regretted." Mr. Grzesch said that his mother had shared many stories with him about his father: of meeting him in a potato field in Poland, of his twirling her on the dance floor to waltzes and polkas, of their scraping together whatever they could to come to America, of his coming home from the Gary Steel Works grimed with soot and sweat. "The stories brought him to life in my imagination," he said, "but no matter how vivid the stories, no matter how precise the details, they could never toss a ball with me or take me to Wrigley Field. In a way, that's what led me to books, so he did make an impact of sorts. If we'd been doing what fathers and sons do, I may never have discovered Twain or Shakespeare or Arthurian legend or Greek mythology. I might not be at this counter with you." He smiled as he brought his mug of coffee to his lips.

I heard the echo of regret in his words, but something else was there, too—appreciation. I couldn't help but think he was grateful for having had a hand in helping me become the man I was becoming. At that counter, for the first time, Mr. Grzesch rose above hero, mentor, and role model; for a moment, a man just seven years my senior felt something like a father. Not in the sense of the man who'd given me life and had battled the earth and elements to provide for my needs; Mr. Grzesch felt like a father who nurtured something that transcended material needs. I could only respond with appreciative silence.

"Speaking of counters," he said, "I love these Saturday lunches, but I was wondering if we might try a change in scenery next week."

"What did you have in mind?" I asked.

"Well," he said, "I was thinking about that first piece you shared with me, the one about your walks with your grandmother and how you continued them after she passed, checking the—what was the German term?"

"*Herrlichkeit*," I said.

"Gesundheit," he laughed. "That's right, the *herrlichkeit*. I've noticed you're less the Chester to my Marshall Dillon anymore, so if your leg is up to it, I wondered if we might check out the *herrlichkeit*. Even though I've lived here for two years, the extent of my authentic landscape experience is driving past it in my Barracuda. Are you game?"

Meg had similarly angled to go on our first walk together,

and for a moment, the full range of sensations from that day returned—the feeling of her hand in mine; the rich smells of autumn mingling with the scent of the last remaining wildflowers; the taste of the beech nuts we shared beneath our tree; the slow melt of kissing her for the first time. Meg inviting herself into my world had thrilled and scared me. The thought of sharing this piece of my world with Mr. Grzesch was different—not thrilling or scary, but worrisome; I wanted him to know me, to see the things I'd written about and help him understand my "how" and "why." He'd helped me answer so many questions over the last two years, but I worried about sharing something that had come to be Meg's and mine with anyone else, even Mr. Grzesch.

We stood on the railroad trestle bridging the mouth of Christy Brook where it spilled into Spiece Lake. "I'm envious," Mr. Grzesch said. "This is part of your regular walk?"

"It is," I said. I understood his envy. The trestle provided one of the best views on the entire walk. The water of the lake was still as held breath that afternoon, a mirror reflecting the blue sky and the white clouds stretched out like cotton balls pulled apart by an inquisitive child, the soaring cedars and white pines, and the fiery oranges and reds of the hardwoods mixed with the evergreens. "When my grandmother was still alive, we'd go down near the water and cut off lengths of pussy willows in the spring and cattails in the fall. She loved bringing them back home and making arrangements in the cut-glass vases that had been her mother's gift to her when she'd left Germany." I pointed to where cattails grew up from the shallow banks of the creek. A soft breeze caused them to sway, their fuzzy brown heads gently tapping as their wide, grassy fronds whispered to each other.

"My mother keeps a small flowerbed behind our row house on the South Side," Mr. Grzesch said, "and as the flowers bloom, she cuts the best stems and hangs them to dry in the basement, near the boiler. Then in the winter months, she puts them all around the house. Lots of yellows and purples. 'They're such regal colors,' she says. It helps her through the winter months."

"I think your mother and my grandmother would have gotten along rather nicely," I said.

"No doubt," he said. "Germans and Poles haven't always exactly broken bread down through history, but from what you've written and told me, I think your grandmother and my mother share something. Our families share something. What brought them here is what makes us the men we are today."

The man had done it again; a week earlier, I'd felt like his symbolic son as we sat at the counter at OJ's Midtown, but now, I felt something different. Between turning eighteen and walking across the stage at graduation, I'd crossed the invisible line that made me a man in the eyes of my country and the letter of the law. My parents saw me differently (despite my father's unspoken desire to have me fall back into certain old roles while living under his roof), and I knew how Meg saw me. But Mr. Grzesch seeing me as a man, articulating it, pushed it past the point of mere knowledge. Perhaps at the fair in August, perhaps before that, we'd ceased being student and teacher. Outside the four walls of his classroom, we still taught and learned, but the labels of teacher and student had fallen away. "Thanks, Mr. Grzesch," I said.

Mr. Grzesch shrugged his shoulders and put on an expression meant to mask that he didn't know what I was talking about, but something in his eyes gave him away. "If you want to thank me for anything, drop that 'mister' thing already and just call me Tom."

"Okay, Tom." My tongue stumbled and the words felt awkward as I replied. Meg and I completed one another; Mr. Grzesch—Tom—had helped me discover I was someone worth completing.

He sensed my awkwardness. "Don't worry, Walt. It's like a new pair of shoes. You just have to break them in. Besides," he said, "I should have had you drop that 'mister' business as soon as Meg's dad handed you your diploma. You earned that right a long time ago."

I laughed, still uncomfortable at using his first name. "You're too kind, Mr. Gr—I mean, Tom."

"Forget about it," he said. He looked down at the cattails growing up around the pussy willows sprouting from the marshy banks where the brook spilled into Spiece Lake. "Those plants growing down there," he said, nodding toward the brook, "I'll be heading back to Chicago for Thanksgiving, and I'd like to bring a little something for my mother. I know she's never seen these, but I think she'd like them. Would it be okay to take some for her, a bit of the Wisconsin woodlands for my city-bound Polish mother?"

"Absolutely," I said. The train bed sloped steeply away from the tracks at the end of the bridge. Descending the bed would test my knee and push the boundaries of the model patient I'd been since the cast had come off. "I'll get you some of the pussy willows, too. No fuzzy white heads like in the springtime, but my grandmother always loved their red bark. She'd put them with cattails in the old, colored glass vases from Germany. After our walks, I'd sit at her table, eating a peanut butter and honey sandwich made with bread she'd baked that morning as she placed the vases around the house and hummed tunes she remembered from when she was a girl."

I reached into my pocket for the knife I was still in the habit of carrying. At the sight of the pocketknife, Tom feigned fear. "I'm glad I'm in present company and not back on the South Side. Someone pulls a knife there, he's not cutting branches."

"An old farm habit," I said. "My grandmother even carried one, this one, in fact. She used it just for this."

"I'd like to have met your grandmother," he said.

"I'd have liked that, too," I said.

"Lead the way, *mon frer*. We're on your turf here."

I took my first step down from the train bed. The small stones crunched beneath my hard-cleated rubber boot sole as I brought down my full weight. Muscles, hip, and most importantly, knee all braced and held. Then I bent my knee, and still supporting my weight, torqued as I brought the other foot down. No pain, and I was still upright. I continued my path down the train bed toward the growth below, each step less deliberate than the one before as bones and muscles remembered tasks they hadn't performed in months, but once reminded of those tasks, they were eager to resume.

When I'd made my way down the long slope and stepped on the spongy ground leading to the banks of Christy Brook, I paused, enjoying the momentary flush of warmth rising in my cheeks followed by the soft sweep of a cool breeze that disappeared almost before it had made itself known. I stepped carefully toward the pussy willows and cattails: not out of apprehension over my knee, but out of a desire not to have a boot full of cold water. I tested the ground with each step, gauging its resistance, its ability to support me before fully planting my weight to take another step. Tom had just reached the bottom of the train bed, and I advised caution. "Wet feet are no fun," I said.

"I'll take your word, Natty Bumppo," Tom said.

"I'd always pictured myself as more of a Chingachgook." I laughed and, taking the final step that brought the plants within my reach, opened the blade of my knife

Tom, stepping tentatively, approached, his movements betraying the fact that he was on unfamiliar turf.

Crouching slightly, I reached out with my left hand, gathering the stalks of several cattails together before closing my fingers and cutting them just above the waterline. I handed them to Tom, who gathered the stalks in his hands and, pulling them close, let the fuzzy brown heads brush his cheek. A boyish look came to his eyes as, grasping the stalks in one hand just beneath the cigar-like flower heads, he traced his index finger over their brown fuzz. We continued, gathering several more spikey stalks topped with large flower heads. Tom cradled them in his arms, an odd bouquet, and drew the flower heads close enough to sniff. "'A remembrancer designedly dropt?'" I asked.

"More than this city boy could have imagined," he said.

I grasped the nearest pussy willow branch between the thumb and index finger of my left hand to steady it. The bark at that time of year was a deep red-brown and was smooth to the touch. With my right hand, I placed the blade of my pocketknife on the opposite side of the stem and braced my thumb so that I could draw the blade into the bark and wood, slicing until I felt the pressure of the blade above the knuckle of my thumb, just before it cut through the last sheath of bark. Pulling my thumb away, I cut through the last bit of bark and placed the stem on the ground beside me.

I continued cutting the branches, a small bundle growing on the patch of earth between Tom and me. He continued examining the cattails, smiling, and in a low voice he spoke to himself. I couldn't make out what he said, but in the snippets that did register as I worked with my knife, I could've sworn he was reciting Whitman.

The bundle of pussy willow branches had grown, the chutes interlocking as the stack grew. "Will this do the trick?" I asked.

"Mom will be beside herself," he said.

"Good," I said. "Just one more." I grasped a branch of the shrub, a bit thicker than the others, and began to draw the blade through. It was more stubborn than the others had been, forcing me to pull the knife with greater force. The blade gathered more momentum than it had in my other cuts, and I was unable to stop it as I had the others. The blade drew through the red bark and my skin. It didn't slice deeply, but it did sink far enough into the ball of my thumb to draw blood. A thin red line, less than a half-inch long, emerged. It didn't hurt, not yet, and Tom, still occupied by the cattails, didn't see what had happened.

For several seconds, I simply watched a thin red line growing, fascinated by the life it possessed. It finally stood out enough for gravity to take over, blood crawling toward the base of my thumb. Pain finally registered, and I shook my hand, sending the pocketknife into the water and drops of my own blood away from me, something I didn't even realize until, reaching toward the shallows to retrieve my knife, I saw a tiny red cloud dissipate, and after pulling my knife out, I saw a faint red smear on a cattail's blade. "Crap," I said, stepping away from the water and balling my hand so that my thumb pressed against my index finger.

"Everything okay?" Tom asked.

"Yeah," I said. "I just nicked my thumb on the knife." I could feel my pulse in my balled hand. I felt foolish. "Won't even need a band-aid."

"Let's see," Tom said.

I opened my hand palm up. A spider's web of blood flowed through the water that had held in the crease of my thumb, then no more red showed, just a pale flap of skin where the blade had cut.

"Hearty northern stock," Tom said. "Knives barely mark you."

I laughed. Still feeling foolish, I stepped away from the water and sat down, opening and closing my hand as though testing all of its joints was somehow necessary given the circumstances. As I sat there, a breeze once again came and went, taking away some of the heat in my cheeks, and I looked back to where I'd been standing. Though the streak was too small to see from where I was seated, I still studied the cattail leaves emerging from the water, searching for my blood and the now dispersed cloud slowly crawling toward the lake. "Did I ever tell you about deer hunting last year?" I asked.

"No, you haven't," said Tom. He set the bundle of cattail spikes down next to the pussy willow branches and took a seat at the base of the train bed. "You've never said much at all about hunting, really. I know you're a hunter, but—"

"I don't know that it's so much about my being a hunter," I said. "But I don't know if I'll be able to take to the woods again after last year…" My voice trailed away, and we let the silence hang between us. The surface of Spiece Lake was no longer glass smooth. Fish-scale ripples of sunlight danced on the water's surface, and I didn't look away as I shared the story with Tom.

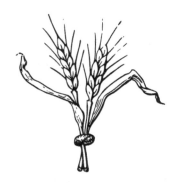

November 18, 1967

MOST YEARS, my father grew antsy as Wisconsin's deer hunting season approached. It was a good kind of antsy, though—nervous excitement. So much about him was so inescapably stern that when he allowed himself to show genuine excitement, it was welcomed by everyone under our roof. Deer hunting genuinely excited my father. He appreciated being in the forest, I know, but not as I did; he did have an affinity for the land, but I knew he wasn't up in his stand reflecting on passages from *Walden*. For him, the hunt offered a different thrill: the opportunity to pit himself against the gray ghosts that haunted the forest. That, added to the satisfaction of providing for his family by putting food on the table, rendered my father as close to intoxicated as any of us would ever witness. A successful hunt satisfied him in ways I could know but not feel until years later.

His customary nervous excitement that fall mixed with a fair measure of crankiness due to an unusual lack of snow. Typically, when the rut began, the bucks' necks swelled beyond normal proportions, and their own hunt clouded their judgment. Snow would already have fallen; never a blizzard, but enough to carpet the fields and fall through the naked canopy of the trees' limbs and cover the forest floor. The absence of that blanket bothered my father, and it showed. In the days before the opener, he muttered under his breath, his not-so-subtle ploy to get whoever was around him to inquire about the mumbling. It was his way of giving the appearance of keeping his irritation under wraps, though we all knew otherwise. My first encounter with his muttering happened in the barn one evening before we began milking. "Lousy background for shooting," he said in a low voice as he forked mounds of corn silage into the manger in front of each cow. He pretended not to notice I was at the other end of the cow, using the business end of a pitchfork to scrape away manure that hadn't quite reached the gutter.

"What's that?" I asked, taking his bait.

He forked another mound of silage. "The brown," he said. "How's a man to draw a proper bead? What if the animal is on the move?" He shook his head. "Your six-pointer last year," he said, "you got him on the run."

"I did," I said. "It wasn't an easy shot, but you're right; the snow helped." We'd tussled over so many other things, I thought I could throw him a bone when it was warranted. I'd started hunting at twelve, part of being a Neumann male, and at 17, I'd yet to experience a hunting season without snow. I could only imagine what my father was fretting about. I wasn't a dedicated hunter in the sense my father would have liked me to be, but the annual gun deer hunt was a family tradition that put food on the table and made my father happy. And though my success in hunting wasn't enough to warrant my father verbalizing his satisfaction with me, it was enough to fend off blunt expressions of disapproval; it aligned with his notion of proper Neumann manhood.

"You've got to be careful, see," he said, bringing the side of his index finger near the tip of his nose before extending his arm fully. "Draw a bead. Line up the post and peep and make certain they're on your target. Nothing worse than a shot that doesn't kill. Cruel. Terribly cruel. And no snow can also make tracking next to impossible..." He left his thought hang as he pushed the rolling steel cart further down the manger and again plunged his five-tined fork into the corn silage.

The week leading up to the opener was full of such moments—for Clay, it was the old tale of the buck that had crossed Christy Brook and would have eluded my father without the faint specks of blood visible on the snow; for my mother, it was his concern that if we didn't hang "at least one big one" from the rafters of the garage, we might have to butcher a steer sooner than we typically did; and for me, it was always the worry over making a good shot on the field. Much of what my father brought up in conversation with me I allowed to go in one ear and out the other—I wasn't all that different from other seventeen year-olds in some ways—but after hearing his concerns enough, those worries began to settle in. I'd shot a deer three of the last four years, had never missed when presented an opportunity, and I had always made clean shots that brought down the animals quickly, mercifully, in plain sight of my stand. Now I wondered. He'd gotten into my head, gotten under my skin in a whole new way. I did my best to laugh it off. Clay, who normally possessed the sternest countenance this side of the old man himself, cracked a smile and rolled his eyes in the wake of one of our father's fits (but only when he knew our father wasn't looking), and I wondered if our father's anxiety had begun getting to him as well.

On the opening day of the hunt, we all awoke much earlier than usual to milk and do chores before marching into the darkness to take our posts in our stands. As they had previous years, the pre-dawn rituals took on an almost ceremonial feel. The routines and patterns of work in the barn were no different than a typical morning's, just earlier, and they were accompanied by eyes that stung a bit more than usual and, in my case, a body that longed to return to the goose-down quilt of my bed and the warmth of the woodstove radiating throughout the old farmhouse. But it being the opener and meaning what it did to my dad, everything was imbued with a different character—not a sense of urgency, but the feeling that accompanies the preparations for any ritual, as though every action and gesture possessed a level of significance not customarily there, as though the very air were charged with a current not strong enough to deliver a jolt, but intense enough to make its presence felt. It remained there all the while we completed our tasks in the barn, and once they'd all been completed, once the rubber boots we all slipped on over Red Wing work boots were hosed clean of manure and barn residue, once we'd come back to the house and thrown off our work coats, another set of rituals began.

As we came through the door into the kitchen, my mother filled our thermoses with steaming coffee that would blaze a trail from lips to stomach as we sat in our stands, cutting through any chill. She spread butter over thick slices of bread she'd baked the night before, then used them to sandwich thumb-thick slices of hickory-smoked ham. I imagined eating my sandwich later; the butter would have turned hard in the refrigeration of Wisconsin in November, and when I chewed, the robust flavor of ham would mingle with the butter warming in my mouth. My mother then wrapped baked goods from Smurawa's Bakery in plastic film, two pastries for each of us. Mine were my favorites, a glazed cruller and a cherry Danish.

My father, Clay, and I quickly and silently ate the breakfast that had been waiting for us: sizzling sausage links that were half-pork, half-venison from the buck I'd shot a year earlier, scrambled eggs peppered just the way my father liked them and mounded in an enameled serving bowl, and mugs of strong coffee to fend off sleep once each of us had settled into our stands in the pre-dawn darkness. We cleared our plates in short order.

Clay and I climbed the groaning stairs to our bedrooms. There, I gave thanks that the chimney passed behind the wall next to my bed, throwing off heat that kept me warm all winter. I took off my barn clothes and hung them from one of the pegs on the strip of molding that ran along the wall at eye level. I slipped into long johns and put on a pair of jeans, thick wool socks, and a heavy flannel shirt. Surveying myself briefly in my mirror, I wondered if my appearance bore any resemblance to one of Jack London's explorers searching for Yukon riches. I stretched, and a yawn escaped me, making me wish for a good long snuggle with Meg rather than tromping off into the cold for the hunt. I reminded myself that she and I had a whole future stretching out ahead of us—a topic we'd first broached earlier that year—and that while I was still living under my parents' roof, I needed to fulfill certain obligations, hunting among them. Besides, I enjoyed the breakfast and farmer sausages, steaks, and hot dogs that came from our venison, especially as they were prepared by my mother.

I tugged the beaded pull chain to turn off the light in my room and stepped into the blue-black hallway. Clay, too, had just left his room and moved through the darkness silently. "Ready to roll?" I asked.

"Affirmative," he said.

We descended the stairs and stepped into the kitchen, where our father had already packed his duffel and was putting on his hunting gear—the same style of red and black Woolrich hunting coat and lined, suspendered pants Clay and I would don in a moment, last Christmas's big present for all the Neumann men.

Clay and I began packing our own duffels. I arranged the contents of mine as if they were three-dimensional puzzle pieces. My glass-lined thermos, the heaviest and largest item, went in first, followed by my field knife (honed to razor sharpness on the whetstone the night before), a box of .30-.30 cartridges, a spare clip, a roll of toilet paper should I need to mark blood spots while tracking, plastic sleeves to slide on my hands and over my arms before field dressing, and a bread bag containing the lunch my mother had packed.

With my duffel set, I pulled on the wool pants over my jeans and adjusted the suspenders before slipping into my coat and Sorel boots. I stuffed my lined buckskin gloves into my coat pockets and removed my rifle from its case, checking the safety before slipping a loaded clip into the hollow just above the trigger guard on the belly of the gun. Like my father and Clay, I levered a cartridge into the firing chamber, the metallic click creating a harsh, quick echo off the yellow painted plaster and stone-tiled floor of the kitchen, and checked the safety once more before ejecting the clip to insert one more cartridge. Loading like that in the kitchen isn't exactly what hunter's safety instructors teach in their classes today, but it was a practice my father insisted upon: "No unnecessary noise when you're out in the field. Silence is always your best friend."

I shouldered my duffel, cradled my rifle, and stepped out of the house. Still no snow, making the pre-dawn darkness all the denser. I could almost feel my father's annoyance rolling back toward me on the puffs of his breath that billowed ghostly white each time he exhaled.

The three of us passed through the yard and beyond the butternut and black walnut trees. I could feel the grass, long crisped by frost, crunch beneath the hard rubber treads of my boots. We moved down the same lane our cows lumbered over on the way to the back pasture where they grazed between milkings in the warmer months. Now, the path was rough, the earth frozen in jagged shapes that refused to yield beneath my weight and wouldn't until the frost had risen from the ground in spring. But for as unforgiving as that path was, it was easy going compared to the plowed soil of the twenty-acre field where Clay and I parted ways with our father. He slid away to the west and north toward his stand, a crow's nest fifteen feet up an old oak overlooking a creek bed that only ran during wet stretches. He moved down an old logging trail we still used to transport firewood each winter on its way home to be split, stacked, and dried in the lean-to woodshed alongside one of my mother's gardens.

Clay and I veered to the east and north, toward my stand, which had been built out of a weathered pallet mounted on a ladder fashioned from the trunks of young jack pine and propped against a sprawling cedar. It gave me a broad view of the field in front of me and a portion of the railroad bed through the border of birch and aspen stretching southward. Though Clay and I had largely followed the furrows created weeks earlier when our father had plowed the field, the walk wasn't easy. My breathing grew heavier as my feet felt their way through the turned earth, and the cold November air stung my lungs as I felt sweat forming beneath the band of my brimmed hunting cap, its earflaps laced up until I settled into my stand.

For Clay, though, movement was a different story. Though our path was rugged, he still moved effortlessly, efficiently, like gliding over the infield dirt to backhand grounders from his position at shortstop. For as much as my brother frustrated me with his reticence and by extension, his approval of all our father said with which I disagreed, I couldn't help but admire the grace of his movement, even so early in the cold November pre-dawn.

We paused upon reaching my stand. The first hint of sunlight rimmed the eastern horizon with a razor-thin slice of gray, and we looked at each other and nodded. Clay still had a quarter-mile to go into the cedar swamp to reach his stand, a shorter version of my ladder stand that gave him a well-camouflaged view of several deer trails converging in a large stand of reed canary-grass. Clay noiselessly disappeared into the forest, somehow maintaining silence while traversing terrain that would make squirrels sound like mythic giants when they stirred with the coming dawn.

Those earliest moments in my stand were the ones I loved most. The world awakened around me, and each year's opening day brought a pleasant surprise. One year, a flock of wild turkeys took off from its roost across the field from me, their wings a low, percussive thump on the air during their cumbersome flight toward me, as though phantom drummers were beating toms in the distance. As they drew closer and passed on either side of me, I felt the *whoosh* of air in their wake. Another year, I'd watched a ruffed grouse emerge from the tall grass bordering field and forest at the foot of my stand. As it walked, the grouse bobbed its head with an odd syncopation, as though the movement somehow afforded it the ability to spot whatever it foraged from the forest floor. When the first insistent squirrel's chatter sounded through the trees, the grouse took off, its flight, like the turkeys', percussive, though its sound was more akin to a quick, tight roll on a snare drum whose wires had been disengaged.

I settled into my stand, sitting on a straw-stuffed woven bag from the feed mill, and looked to the east, between the silhouettes of birch and aspen and across the railroad tracks to the horizon where the first pinks and oranges were now painting the sky. The scene made me think of Meg; we'd shared more than one sunset, but never a sunrise. I added that to the mental checklist of the thousand-and-one things we'd promised to one day do together, and I wished that she were there with me sharing the moment—the clouds on the horizon were dyed more colors than I imagined possible, and I wondered how this tableau would look on canvas if Meg were to capture it in one of her paintings.

I shivered as the sun crept above the horizon. The cold had reached the light sweat I'd worked up hiking to my stand. I untied the strings holding up my earflaps and pulled them down. Birds were coming to life as if emerging from the air itself, sparrows and nuthatches and shrill blue jays flitting from tree limb to tree limb. A chickadee landed on the barrel of my rifle lying across my lap, then perched on my knee before again taking flight and blending into the stillness of the air. *A good sign,* I thought, registering the almost imperceptible force of its take-off from my knee. Such good fortune, I reasoned, warranted acknowledgment. I un-cinched the drawstring of my duffel hanging from a limb to my right and reached in for the cruller, anticipating its sweet crumble of glaze and pastry. I was careful to make my movements as silent as possible. Just as my hand pulled the cruller from the bag, I caught movement to my left in the periphery of my vision.

I set down the pastry on top of the bag and slowly swiveled for a better look. A deer, or the shadow of one, moved like a phantom whose borders were imprecise but whose matter was there, of one substance with its surroundings while simultaneously free of them. My heart skipped a beat, and a torrent of thoughts, most of them planted by my father, stormed my brain: was it a buck or a doe? No doe tags this year. Stay quiet. Move slowly. Why couldn't the sun be just a bit higher? *If only there'd been snow...*

I deliberately reached beneath my coat sleeve and pulled back the cuff of my glove. The faint green luminescence of my watch's hands read 6:30. It was legal to shoot. I breathed deeply and squinted at the ghost out on the field. Its head was low to the ground; it must have been looking for any remnants of corn still there after picking and plowing. When it raised its head, I saw a momentary glint: sunlight on polished antler. A buck. That glint gave me corrective lenses that brought the world into focus. The ghostly borders of his silhouette now had a degree of definition. His neck was swollen to almost twice its normal size. Shadow became substance as his antlers now stood out. Given the lighting and lack of snow as a backdrop, I couldn't be certain, but they looked like those of the buck my father had described after flushing it from the cornfield while picking earlier that fall. His sighting was brief, he said, little more than a glimpse, but the accuracy of my father's mental snapshots was typically precise. His description came to life as, still squinting, I studied the creature. Heavy main beams stretched well past the tips of its ears. Brow tines stood nearly a foot above the beams. My father's voice sounded in my head—*Biggest buck I've seen. Ever*—and he wasn't a man given to hyperbole.

But for as distinct as some features were, the deer's transformation was incomplete, and I questioned whether what I was seeing was the product of my senses or wishful thinking. Three filled Neumann tags would mean the end of the hunt. I might even be able to go back to school on Monday, a thought that would have horrified my father. School before hunting? Blasphemy! I shifted in my stand, not wanting to alert the deer, who at more than one hundred yards away was still oblivious to my presence as he poked his nose into the furrows of frozen soil. I moved my left hand to the stock of my rifle and grasped its butt with my right, just shy of the trigger. I raised my left foot to the step nailed just below the pallet, allowing me to use my knee as a prop on which I steadied my rifle. I placed my index finger inside the trigger guard, rested the rifle's stock across my knee, and brought the butt to my shoulder, tipping my head slightly to draw a bead. The oiled metal's iciness against my cheek felt several degrees colder than the air temperature. I swallowed hard and took a deep breath. My dad's voice again came to me: *Calm, Walt. Calm and steady. Peep and post and draw a bead just back of the front shoulder. Wait. Peep, post, shoulder. Make sure. You don't want to...no snow, remember...be certain, Walt. Be very, very certain. Now the safety. When you're ready, just squeeze...*

And in the infinitesimal instant between my decision to fire and its being carried across nerve endings to my right index finger, another hunter, a neighbor acres away, fired a shot at a target of his own. The buck I'd done my best to sight in without spooking spun as I squeezed the trigger and leaped toward the narrow stand of birch and aspen separating the field and the railroad tracks, to the east, toward the sun crawling high enough to erase the soft pinks and oranges with a harsher, colder light. And as the deer strode, I detected a slight hitch in his movements; as he alternated between arcing bounds and short sprints so characteristic of whitetails, I sensed something in his gait. But whether that something was owing to my shot having hit him or the difficulty of moving on a plowed, frozen field, I couldn't tell.

Deer I'd shot previously left no question of my having hit the mark. Their impact was swiftly apparent in each case, the deer buckling, rising for perhaps an awkward stride or two, then collapsing to the earth. My father had been an expert marksman in the army, and he liked to attribute my marksmanship to my having inherited it from him. But the deer that morning, the heavy-browed buck who so excited my father weeks earlier, neither buckled nor collapsed. Unable to re-position my sights on his bounding form, I didn't fire a second shot. He disappeared, over the old barbed-wire fence marking the boundary between the field and the strip of birch and aspen, and then, I could only guess, down the embankment to the railroad tracks, and from there, I couldn't say.

My heart dropped twice after the rush of adrenaline that accompanied the shot and left me quivering like a leaf clinging to a limb in the face of approaching winter. It dropped first at the thought of my father, the disappointment and the cold shoulder I'd endure prior to his meticulously dissecting and questioning every one of my thoughts and actions leading up to the shot.

It dropped a second time at the thought of the deer, possibly wounded, making its way to wherever a wounded whitetail went. I wondered if it might suffer. I wondered if it might pull through. I wondered if I'd even hit it at all. The only certainties at that moment were my own uncertainty and the heavy, sick feeling pulling down on the floor of my stomach.

My cruller, one of Smurawa's finest, was still sitting on top of my duffel, but I'd lost any desire to eat it. And with the post gun-fire adrenaline rush gone, I became aware of the cold once again creeping in with greater intensity than it had earlier, starting at the tips of my fingers and toes and working its way up my limbs toward my core.

With shaking fingers, I placed the cruller back in the bread bag and fumbled for my thermos, my efforts to remain quiet failing miserably. The metal clips fastening the handle to the body of the thermos rattled as I unscrewed the lid and stopper to pour the hot, black liquid. Steam rose from the lid that doubled as a cup, and I drank deeply, not caring that the coffee burned my tongue; I wanted to chase away the cold creeping in. The coffee worked for that task, but it couldn't peel away the cold fingers of anxiety clutching me.

I remembered what my dad had always advised in the event of wounding a deer—*give it time. Don't leave your stand right away, like some hunters do. Hold off on checking for any sign of blood. You can always track the animal, and what some wounds do is kill a deer through internal bleeding. Too many hunters want to track right away, and they end up rousting the animal, pushing it for miles until all the bleeding is internal and they completely lose the track. A wounded deer wants two things: to bed down and to drink water.* So I continued sitting in my stand, drinking coffee, trying to calm myself with my father's words. I checked my watch. Ten minutes since I'd shot. I gave the cruller another chance, but I couldn't taste it. Same with the cherry Danish. I checked my watch again. A half-hour. Not long enough, so I kept waiting, watching the birds and squirrels from my perch, hearing shots fired by other hunters elsewhere, not wanting to have to share my story and risk embarrassment if I had hit the deer but was unable to find it. I drank more coffee and felt the urge to relieve myself. I made a final check of my watch. An hour had passed since I fired the single shot, and I decided to leave my stand. With my duffel slung over one shoulder and my rifle in my right hand, I climbed down the ladder. When I stepped off the final rung, I saw the spent cartridge from my shot, and I picked it up from the ground. I pocketed the cartridge along with my gloves and began undoing zippers.

With my bladder no longer protesting, I put my gloves back on and was about to take my first step toward the field when a voice said, "Boo." Clay, from a crouched position behind the trunk of the tree against which my stand was propped, stood with something resembling a smirk on his face.

I flinched at the surprise of hearing another voice. "What are you doing?" I asked.

"I thought you might need a hand," he said.

"Need a hand?" I asked.

"With your deer," he said. "One shot's a sure thing, and with your reputation as the next Wild Bill Hick—"

I cut him off. "I wish that were the case," I said. "I don't know if I hit him or not."

"Big one?"

"Remember the one that got the old man so hyped up a few weeks back?"

"Really?" he said.

"I think so," I said.

"What happened?" he asked.

I told him about seeing the buck in the low light, checking the time, the brief flash of antler bringing things into focus, the other shot, the spin, the possible hitch in the deer's gait.

"That's a pisser," Clay said.

"I feel sick," I said.

"You did just take a rather monumental piss," he said.

"One has nothing to do with the other," I said.

"I know," Clay said. "Half a thermos of coffee has that effect."

"Just how long have you been hiding out behind my tree?"

Clay smiled. "Awhile," he said. "I'd only been in my stand ten or fifteen minutes before I heard you shoot, so I figured, 'what the hell? If he's got one laying on the field, it'll be a bugger dragging it over that frozen mess.' Plus, it's good practice for me."

"Practice?" I asked.

"You didn't know I was there, did you?"

I shook my head. "Practice?" I asked again.

Clay shook his head. "Never mind."

Neither of us said anything. "You think we've waited long enough?"

"I think so," he said.

"No sign of Dad," I said.

"I didn't expect there would be," he said. "You know him—the patience of Job—and if we've got something happening here on our end, he'll want us to take care of it. Brotherly bonding. Manly fortitude. Pulling ourselves up by our own bootstraps."

What Clay said was true. We knew his lines.

"Let's check things out," I said.

"Lead the way," Clay replied.

We walked to the spot in the field where I approximated the deer had been when I shot. We both studied the dark, tilled soil, searching for a spot of red or a tuft of hair, but against the muted palette of Wisconsin farmland, neither showed itself.

"And he headed east?" Clay asked. They would be the last words he would speak to me for some time.

"Yup," I said moving toward where the buck had jumped the barbed-wire fence.

When the deer had leapt, it appeared graceful, its jump an elegant parabola, a momentary escape from gravity. I told Clay about its stride when running, that I sensed something out of the ordinary. He nodded, motioning with one hand for me to lower my volume, his eyes never looking at me, but instead sweeping the ground before us. I kept an eye on the field as well, but before long, everything I scanned in my proximity blurred together. Clay stopped at the fence, and bending at the waist, looked at the rusted barbed-wire. He motioned for me to join him. Now crouching, he pointed at the sagging top strand of the barbed-wire. Barely visible on the rusted braid was a small, scarlet drop, and a tuft of no more than five or six white hairs. I'd hit my target, but if the sign we'd found were any indicator, I hadn't hit it well—or I'd made the dreaded "gut shot," which meant the deer could go and go and go before expiring, leaving scant sign of its path with the lack of snow compounding the difficulty of tracking. Clay reached into his duffel and tore off a square of toilet paper to impale on a barb near blood and hair before handing me the roll and motioning for me to follow him.

He stepped over the sagging fence and went on, silently and deliberately moving through the forty-foot wide wooded border between field and railroad track. I went with him, ten feet to his left and a step or two behind him, looking, as he did, at the ground, littered with leaves, hoping to spot another tuft of hair or drop of blood, but to no avail. Clay, however, upon reaching the spot where the ground dropped away in a steep slope higher than either of us were tall, surveyed that drop-off in longer and longer sweeps until he found it—a smear of blood no larger than a quarter on a brown-speckled yellow birch leaf. I placed another square of toilet paper at the spot on a naked, pencil-thin branch above the leaf and looked back at the first marker. The deer, in moving toward the tracks, had begun drifting northward—angling toward water, I thought, as Spiece Lake lay three-quarters of a mile to our north, fed by Christy Brook, whose waters moved swiftly enough to fend off frost. Clay and I descended the embankment to the tracks, moving along the imaginary line suggested by the two faint signs my brother had found.

We continued our search in that fashion for nearly three hours. I diligently sought any sign of the wounded animal's path, but with no luck. Always, it was Clay who spotted the pin-prick of blood and I who marked the spot. At times, we might go for a quarter- or half-hour without finding anything, prompting us to return to the last marker and strike a slightly different trajectory than we'd imagined the deer taking, and invariably, Clay's instincts proved correct. We moved carefully, stepping lightly. I feared that my next step might obliterate whatever scant evidence of passage the deer may have left. More than once I was ready to give up entirely, my sense of apparent hopelessness outweighing the guilt I felt at imagining a magnificent creature I'd wounded dying somewhere and having to share such a humiliating story with my father, Mr. Grzesch, and Meg. To have kept such a story to myself, or to have my brother relate it to his friends and have it find the ears of those who mattered to me, would have shamed me more than telling it myself.

Clay, though, was dogged. His movements over a varied landscape were efficient and silent, whether we moved over unplowed fields or through patches of scrub forest, along the bed of the Chicago Northwestern rails, or through the partially frozen lowlands that occasionally gave way beneath my weight but which held for Clay's lighter tread. For as terrible as I felt, I grudgingly came to admire what my brother was doing, to respect that what I was witnessing was as much a gift as his talent on the diamond.

The only time I found myself unwilling to defer to him was when the deer's route seemed headed toward the meadow. My brother's every instinct had been correct, had been the sole reason we'd kept finding sparse signs of the deer; whether I instinctively knew that the animal couldn't have crossed into the opening of the meadow or I was merely hoping against hope,

I wasn't about to let this journey go there. Clay had reached a fork on a deer path we were following and had taken his first step down the left branch, the branch that would have, in fifty feet, spilled into the meadow, when I hissed his name in a hoarse whisper. He paused, then pivoted to meet my stare. I shook my head and mouthed *no*. Clay raised his eyebrows, questioning me. I again shook my head, more emphatically this time, then tilted my head toward the right branch.

Clay silently mouthed, *are you sure?*

I nodded, and my brother motioned for me to take the lead. For a moment, I felt a sense of relief and sent a silent *thank you* to anyone eavesdropping on my thoughts. I looked back through the naked branches and caught a glimpse of the last toilet paper marker we'd placed, barely stirring in the breeze some hundred feet back. I took a deep breath and exhaled before I stepped down the right branch, a branch I knew from my walks would soon bring us to a creek feeding Christy Brook.

I drew from an imagined well of fortitude to re-up my focus, and at the spot where the trail began to veer away from the meadow, on the moss-covered base of a maple, a patch of frost had encrusted the delicate frilled edges of the moss, and in the middle of that patch was a single red drop. I paused, astonished at my good fortune, and tore a square of toilet paper from the roll.

Clay, now standing beside me, also saw the spot and gave me a congratulatory clap on the shoulder. A few feet further down the path was more blood, a larger smear the length of a loaf of bread, and several strides beyond that, another smear against the trunk of a tree, and I knew. For an instant, I forgot about embarrassment and shame and trepidation. For an instant, I felt I'd done something right. For an instant, I imagined my father's praise, and an energy coursed through me, enough to allow me to find the deer I was now certain had given up the ghost and with my brother's help, drag it back to the field. From there, we'd tromp home for the tractor and bring it to hang from the rafters of the garage, where it would chill and firm overnight, allowing us to skin it with relative ease the next afternoon and quarter the carcass before boning and trimming the meat as we all stood around the kitchen table.

For an instant.

Then I heard the snort and the thrashing.

Clay and I moved toward the sound. The deer lay in a shallow depression ringed by scrub cedars. When I first saw him, he again took on the ghostly qualities I'd witnessed on the field, but as my eyes took in the sight, my brain processed the scene. He lay on his side, his head rising on his swollen neck, and despite every effort he made to gather his legs beneath him and stand, he couldn't; he flailed, his breath coming out in short, violent bursts that became clouds of vapor in the cold air. My shot had clipped his stomach—not a wound that produced much external bleeding, not a wound that killed quickly. It was enough of a wound to bring him to the edge of death, to let his own strength and the tragic beauty of his own instincts and locomotion hasten his demise.

The wound was almost enough, and I'd inflicted it.

As he'd headed toward cover and water, the combination of

his own movement and the force of gravity pulling on his bowels had opened the wound further. He'd probably bedded more than once over the course of the looping trek he'd taken, and I'm certain we had—or more accurately, I had, as Clay may as well been a phantom moving along the route—stirred him from those beds, pushed him further, until, in reaching the depression where he now writhed, nothing could hold. I saw his bowels spilling onto the ground, the milky gray stomach and coiled intestines with the burnt orange flecks of fallen, dried cedar greens clinging to them. My own stomach lurched, and a gorge rose to burn the back of my throat with the taste of wood smoke.

And though I managed to choke it back, I could not prevent my heart from dropping a third and final time that day when Clay spoke. I couldn't make out everything he said; it came in snippets, but the longest phrase I recall was clear as a bell, perhaps because it echoed a voice in my own head: "you know what to do." But while I now know it was my brother's voice, that day, in that moment, in the wash of white noise filling my brain, I couldn't distinguish between Clay and my father. I froze. *Single shot,* the voice said. *To the neck.* The deer's head swung toward me, and we briefly made eye contact—maybe for a second, maybe for several seconds, but it felt like ages compressed in an instant, as though someone or something were trying to speak with me through my brother or the animal. Perhaps both. Whoever or whatever it was, it was broadcasting on an existential frequency I couldn't triangulate. *End it,* the voice said.

I felt my consciousness floating outside my body, bearing witness to my actions, or lack of them, watching myself at the same time I tried to will myself to act, to raise the rifle to my shoulder, to align peep and post and swollen neck of the deer, to slip my trembling index finger through the trigger guard and flick the safety to off with my thumb, to squeeze the trigger and mercifully end the life of the handsome creature flailing on the ground, its very self spilling out before me—*Walt?*—and I felt as though I were being watched, watched not only by some part of myself and by my brother, but also by my father and mother, by Meg and her parents, by Rev. Stubenvoll and Mayor Lambrecht and Thomas Lindow, by every teacher I'd ever had, from wrinkled old Mrs. Melchoir on up to Mr. Grzesch himself—*Walt!*—by Mark Raddatz and Eilene Ehlers and a toddler I'd never seen, a young girl in a Winnie the Pooh jumper with an inquisitive look in her bright, brown eyes, and they all watched me and willed me to act in some fashion, to walk away from either the task I knew was right or the one I felt was right.

I couldn't perform either one. I froze.

I stood in one place, my rifle half-raised. A cold bead of sweat trickled down my rib cage, and my feet felt like they were encased in concrete. My hands and arms wanted to move, but something inside me held them in check. I wanted to at least turn my head away, to search for sunlight flashing through the cedar boughs, but I couldn't. I couldn't move, couldn't speak, couldn't give any indicator of hearing or heeding the exhortations, real or imagined, flying toward me or swirling within me—but I could see my brother to my right, his expression somewhere between placidness, disgust, and pity as he raised his rifle, took aim, and fired the killing shot.

April 1, 1969

MEG AND I were part of the crowd stretching away
from the statue of Abraham Lincoln on Bascom Hill
as speakers of various stripes riled protestors, giving them an
outlet for their anger and indignation. It had been our second
protest that week, and though we'd been participating in such
demonstrations since the semester had begun, neither of us
had come to feel entirely comfortable at these events. Not for
lack of trying. We wanted to wave signs and shout and chant
with abandon, to add our voices to a chorus venting righteous
indignation and force change through the strength of will and
sheer numbers. Since arriving in Madison, I'd more than ever
come to hate the war and anyone responsible for propagating
it. While protesting, though, I never felt passion burning like

a hot coal through the floor of my stomach; protest fueled my intellect, and the protests were a matter of principle. They'd become a necessary exercise in bridging the gulf between intellect and emotion.

My desire to lose myself in the sweep of such events was tempered, to some degree, by my hometown and upbringing. Some of it I attributed to the conversations Tom and I had had before I left Gillett, talks about simultaneously hating the war and supporting the men actually fighting it. Some of it was nested in the knowledge that after graduating from high school that spring, my brother Clay would enlist and throw himself headlong into his goal of serving America as a Screaming Eagle. Hate the war and love the soldier. Despite the fact this particular soldier-to-be's stance royally pissed me off, blood still mattered.

When Meg and I protested, even our protest signs failed to blend in. Hers were legitimate works of art, bearing witness to her artistic sensibility, marked as much by her awareness of line and form, of composition and arrangement, as by her opposition to Vietnam. Often, Meg's signs were inspired by pieces she was studying in her courses. In February, she'd spent hours with pen and ink creating a sign resembling an 18th century print entitled "Gin Lane" by William Hogarth. Hogarth included an undertaker who will be kept busy tending to the casualties of Gin Lane; Meg included General Westmoreland directing coffins down a ramp from the cargo bay of a military transport. Hogarth included a jester dancing amid the chaos and ruin around him; Meg included Ho Chi Minh doing the Frug. And Hogarth prominently featured a prostitute covered by syphilitic sores dropping an infant to its death; Meg foregrounded a bloated Uncle Sam dropping babies diapered in jungle fatigues into an abyss. On her sign for April Fool's Day, she'd used acrylics to create a modern version of Pieter Bruegel's "The Triumph of Death": skeletal dogs scavenging a razed Vietnamese village amid corpses and smoking ruins, a cart full of skulls drawn by a gaunt horse led by President Nixon. Though I encouraged Meg to keep these signs, she never did; they either made their way to the trash barrel on our way back to the dorm or were given to a fellow protestor who asked her for them.

On my signs, I used simple block text to make literary allusions that elicited polite head-scratching if they attracted any attention at all. Except that day. I'd scrawled four lines whose sad irony I loved: "My friend, you would not tell with such high zest / To children ardent for some desperate glory, / The old Lie: *Dulce et decorum est / Pro patria mori.*" As the final speaker at the protest concluded his remarks, I held the sign aloft amid the raucous cheering, and when I did, I heard a voice situated somewhere between Leonard Cohen and John Wayne meant for me. "Hot damn, young man. Nothing like resurrecting the ghosts of the past to speak to the present."

"What was that?" I asked, looking in the direction of the voice.

"That sign," he said. "Goddamn Wilfred Owen. Could've used a healthy dose of him in my field manual." The man speaking wore a long, olive-drab overcoat, and he hadn't shaved in weeks, the red of his beard matching the tendrils snaking from beneath a black wool skullcap. He reminded me of an irate Lucky

Charms leprechaun torn from his world of magical marshmallows. "Owen calls on Horace, and here you blow the dust off the old Limey. You must actually crack a book every now and again. Good for you, Junior." He clapped my shoulder, his hand blunt as granite through my jacket.

The crowd had begun breaking up, groups of people improvising their own chants as they scattered in all directions. Meg grabbed my arm and held tight. "It's cold, Walt." Though she wore a heavy coat, I felt the shiver passing through her.

"Good plan," I said. "Sunroom?"

"Perfect." Meg's smile ended her brief spell of teeth chattering.

We started for State Street, and I turned to the man who'd commented on my sign. As he shifted from one foot to the other, hugging himself, Tom's voice came to mind. "One second," I said to Meg, then asked the grubby leprechaun, "Would you like a warm drink?"

"A literate mind reader," he said. "I'd be foolish to turn down such kindness."

Meg tugged at my sleeve, and her expression asked what was happening. I returned an *it's okay* look, and she nodded.

The three of us exchanged introductions on the walk to State Street, the dome of the State Capitol looming over the city and everyone in it, and made our way up the long flight of stairs to the Sunroom Café. Upon opening the door, a warm rush of mingled scents washed over us—minestrone and pastries, strong coffee, grilling sausage, pungent Asian spices and ginger. Meg and I moved toward our favorite spot, a small table near a window overlooking the stream of pedestrians below, and pulled over a third chair for our guest, Tyler. Our waitress, her hands covered by intricate henna tattoos, brought us menus and took our order for a bottomless pot of coffee. When she returned with the coffee, Meg and I ordered our food—Meg, the grilled chicken salad, and I, the pasta with sausage and fresh mozzarella. Tyler held up his hand, indicating coffee would be enough for him, but I invited him to order as well. He looked skeptical, but I insisted. "They pay me the big bucks at the University Bookstore," I said, "just so I can treat strangers to dinner. Besides, you're looking a bit hungry."

"Your call," he said and ordered the crispy Thai peanut noodle bowl without hesitation. There in the café, his coat now hanging from the back of his chair but his black skullcap still clinging to his head, Tyler was no longer as wired as he'd been on Bascom Hill. He drank his coffee purposefully, drawing from his mug as though the steaming liquid had no effect on his tongue or throat, and slumped in his chair as he scanned the room systematically, only breaking his patterned surveillance for sounds rising above the general hum, a mug clinking especially loudly against a saucer, a plate crashing in the kitchen, a diner emphasizing a point emphatically.

To say that a level of discomfort existed between the three of us would be an understatement. Meg and I were accustomed to having entire conversations without saying a word, but Tyler threw everything out of balance. We attempted the customary pleasantries, but Tyler's muttered responses either bore an edge I was reluctant to press or a cryptic character that puzzled me.

Me: "What brought you here today?"

Tyler: "That should be rather apparent, no?"

Meg: "Do you think these rallies are making a difference?"

Tyler: "For the benefit of Mr. Kite, there will be a show tonight."

Me: "Is Madison home for you?"

Tyler: "I was 'round when Jesus Christ / had his moment of doubt and pain. / Made damn sure Pilate / washed his hands and sealed his fate."

Not until our orders arrived and I made the offhand comment that Tyler seemed to enjoy his Thai dish did he come to life. "I can taste it," he said.

Meg furrowed her brow. "Taste what?" she asked.

Tyler smiled, his expression disbelieving but with a maniacal edge. "Vietnam, of course."

I spoke. "But aren't you having Thai—"

"Smart boys shouldn't ask obvious questions," he said, "or did you bum that sign from someone else?"

For a moment, I felt as though I were back in Tom's classroom, though when Tom pressed me, it had never felt like an attack. "So what does Vietnam taste like?" I asked.

Tyler smacked his lips and smiled. "Not bad, smart boy. Good starting point." He closed his eyes for several seconds before speaking. "It tastes like a thousand things," he said. "It's nuac mam from a barrel of fermented anchovies on the sidewalk in Saigon. It's cheap whiskey on the lips of a bar girl in Danang. It's the filth of a rice paddy that doubles as a ville's latrine. It's the emptiness you force down your gullet when you're pulling pieces of a kid from Nebraska from the bamboo after he steps on a bouncing Betty. And it's the green M&M's the medic keeps tucked away for when the shit really hits the fan." Tyler was looking at me, but I felt he was seeing someone, or something, else, not really over my shoulder, but behind me, as though he were staring through me at an indeterminate point in the distance. I felt a chill and reached for my coffee.

For what felt like several minutes but couldn't have been longer than a few seconds, we sat there. Meg lowered the forkful of romaine and grilled chicken she'd been about to place in her mouth. Tyler snorted. "The culinary tour of Vietnam for cherries. Still hungry, friends?" He finished the last of his noodle bowl. "So why aren't you humping it in Southeast Asia?" he asked me. "Mommy and Daddy have enough cash to send you to school and get you a college deferment? Or did you score one of those precious spots in the National Guard?"

His words hit me—not so much for what they said, but for the condescension that reminded me of Clay's venom in August—and for an instant, anger roiled in my stomach. I didn't take his bait, however. Meg appeared concerned, but I gave her a *stay calm* look and drew a deep breath. "None of the above," I said, then gave the thumbnail of the medical deferment allowing me to attend the university. He continued staring through me, but I sensed him taking in every word. As I finished, Meg gave my forearm a squeeze.

"Lucky bastard," Tyler quipped. "What I wouldn't have done for a million dollar hangnail." He'd again come to life, riding the same wave I'd sensed back on Bascom Hill, and he told us his own story, stopping only to punctuate anecdotes with long draws of coffee or to motion our waitress to refill the pot. He'd grown up on his family's cattle ranch in Ada, Oklahoma and had gone to Oklahoma University in Norman after high school. He majored in philosophy (to his father's chagrin) and participated in the ROTC program (at his father's insistence), and shortly after graduating, he was commissioned as a lieutenant in the United States Army. Less than a year later, he was leading a platoon from the 1st Battalion of the 23rd American Infantry Division in the Quang Ngai Province.

When he dropped that tidbit, he looked at me as if testing me. I passed. "You can't be serious," I said.

Tyler looked at Meg. "You've got a smart one." Then, he looked at me. "As a heart attack, kid. I wasn't part of Charley Company, thank God. I don't even want to think of what I might've done had I been with those boys. My unit cleaned up the mess, though. That's one seriously fucked-up shit hole."

"Tell me more about that shit hole," I said.

For the next hour, Tyler shared Vietnam stories, and as he did, Meg and I saw him go through a range of emotions. When describing the sunsets over the calm, South China Sea, he was placid and serene, as though he wished to remain suspended in the pinks, oranges, and blues. When describing hordes of children shouting "G.I. number one! G.I. number one!" and begging for American chocolate, he went cold and said that he and his platoon knew that after getting the chocolate, the children would talk to the VC. He told us about the totems men carried and the souvenirs they collected: the pantyhose of a girlfriend stateside; the snapshots of family, friends, and lovers; the baseball glove one private clutched to his chest as he dreamed, his legs twitching as though wanting to run and run and run; the ears and thumbs secreted away in the bottom of rucksacks along with the fleeting, eternal fury, confusion, and desperation that prompted the bearers of such tokens to slice them away in the first place.

His words alternately dripped rancor and desperation when he told us about Hill 508, of taking it three times over the course of four days, each time abandoning it, leaving him to wonder what the purpose had been in two of his men dying on that hill. "Goddamn cluster fuck," he said. So many anecdotes involved death, and when he spoke of it, he sounded older than he appeared. In being exposed to death and in vast quantities—deaths of soldiers he knew, deaths of civilians chalked up as "collateral damage," or the death of the occasional, elusive Viet Cong—he claimed to have been numbed to it, desensitized, and we bore witness to how his very words had metamorphosed death itself. For Tyler, the dead didn't have names. They were "crispy critters" and "crunchy munchies," and somehow they didn't die, not really. Instead, they "kicked the bucket" or "bought the farm" or "caught a Freedom Bird out of Indian Country."

Tyler's final Vietnam story involved a young soldier from Wisconsin named Paul. "I felt for him," he said. "Farm kid. Could tell he was scared shitless those first weeks. I took him under my wing. Had to. The others would have been merciless on his innocent little self. Paul gave new meaning to the term 'cherry.' When he wasn't scared, he was fascinated by the rice paddies and the animals. Awfully damned fond of water buffalos. We'd be humping through a ville—story of our lives, that endless fucking humping—and I'm supposed to keep everything tight, textbook SOPs, but here and there, Paul just drifts, stroking the nose of a buffalo or tugging up rice to study the roots. I had to keep him close so I could reel his ass in. He was better after a couple of weeks, but I could still sense him wanting to drift. At night, when we'd set up camp, everyone else is talking shit, playing cards or writing letters, maybe hunker down to smoke a joint, but Paul digs in and he pulls out his bag of corn. I kid you not. Plastic bread bags tripled up and filled with hard yellow kernels 'from back home,' as he put it. He'd sit there with his hand shoved in, just moving them around, almost like he's looking for something. Other times he'd pop one into his mouth and roll it over his tongue. Sometimes, he'd plant one of those kernels like he's the Johnny frickin' Appleseed of the Vietnam peninsula. Strange, but no stranger than other things I've seen." Tyler paused, as if measuring just how to phrase his next thought. "The thing is, those damn kernels are what scared the shit out of me, brought me here today."

Tyler tapped his mug with a spoon, the *ting* sharp against the sounds of the café, and studied the tablecloth before looking back up at me. Meg looked at me questioningly. This wasn't what she'd anticipated when she suggested warming up at the Sunroom and I invited Tyler to join us. I lowered my chin and knitted my eyebrows, gesturing to wait on what Tyler would say next. She took a deep breath and looked out the window. Meg was the most patient and understanding person I knew, but I wondered if where Tyler had taken us was too much for her. He was pushing even my envelope, but I wanted him to finish his story. "You're in Wisconsin to find Paul?" I asked.

"Among other things," Tyler said. He hunched as if trying to make himself smaller. "Paul had been in-country for a month, and I was a short-timer at that point. I just wanted to ride it out, notching my stick and waiting to catch a bird back to the world, but we get caught in a real shit storm. Middle of the monsoon season of course. Some little dink I'd given chocolate probably gave away our location. Not yet dawn, can't see squat, air's thick enough to chew. My boys are going nuts, firing into the darkness. God only knows what the hell they're shooting at. All I can see are tracers and quick flashes from their mortars and the claymores on the perimeter. Rounds from their AKs are zipping past, so I find the RTO and call in arty. I send the coordinates—couldn't just sit on my ass. Had to make things warm for someone on the receiving end of all that ordnance. And for a while, that jungle lit up like you wouldn't believe. And the wicked sound! Their firing on us was Peter, Paul, and Mary compared to Uncle Sam's Jimi Hendrix. After we drop some National fuckin' Anthem on them, after all that firepower, then comes the quiet. Only sound is the rain. I'm checking to make sure I still have all my parts, just like everybody else in the platoon, then everyone starts talking shit, like they're the biggest swingin' dicks in all of Southeast Asia. Only there's no Paul; kid's nowhere, so we fan out. Dawn's breaking, and I'm expecting to find his shit blown halfway to Hanoi. I'm half-composing a letter in my head for his parents when I come across him. He's sitting on the trunk of a fallen tree swinging his feet and whistling. He's got that damned bag of corn in one hand, plucking kernels out of it with the other, pinching them between his thumb and index finger and throwing them, kind of like you'd throw a dart. 'Hey, Paul,' I say, 'where the hell you been?'

"Sonofabitch doesn't turn around. Just keeps tossing kernels. I step into the clearing and see what's across from him. There's a dead VC sitting with his back against a tree and the top of his skull caved in. No sign of the big stuff; no burns, no missing limbs. Just that bashed-in skull, and I can see the water pooling in there. And here's the kicker: every few seconds, a kernel of corn plops in—sploosh...sploosh...sploosh. Finally, Paul turns around—blood spatter across the bridge of his nose and on his hands. 'Air's clearer out here, lieutenant,' he said.

"'What the hell?' I say to myself. There he was. Just whistling and swinging his feet, tossing corn into a VC skull. I tried talking with him. Asked him about the shit storm, what he'd done. No response. I tried big and scary, tried buddy-buddy. Nada. Not a peep, not what he'd seen or done, or why he was tossing kernels of Wisconsin corn into the bashed-in skull."

Meg was still looking out the window toward the street below, crying. She turned to Tyler. "So what did you do?" she asked.

Tyler squinted, gauging her before he continued. He looked at me and raised an eyebrow. I held Meg's hand and nodded. He continued, his voice lower. "We were supposed to report back to base camp in two days, so I just kept the kid close. Damned if I knew what he might do. I wasn't letting him out of my sight. He didn't act any differently those two days. Back at base camp, I wrote up what happened in the sticks and recommended him for evaluation. The boys called him in, and that was the last I saw of him. But for the rest of my time there, I couldn't shake that image of him in the clearing. Still can't. Got under my skin. Wondered what made a kid who liked petting water buffalos' noses cross the line." Tyler shook his head and drained his mug. "Why do any of us? What if I'd been with the 123rd in My Lai? I'm human, though—you know what I mean? I needed to hold someone accountable. I started thinking it through. Didn't know the kid's background, so it's hard to point fingers at mommy and daddy or bullies on the playground. Maybe a DI in Basic failed him, didn't bust his chops and build him back up into a bigger, better, badder version of himself. Maybe a character flaw—didn't have the cojones to handle the fucked-up shit a nineteen year-old grunt faces in the jungle.

"I mean, all of that's part of it, but I wasn't satisfied. So I starting asking the big questions. My professors in college would have been proud. Causation, right? I've got to pin this shit down. So I'm hashing through them all—Plato and Aristotle, Thomas and Hume and Locke—and after a while, my head's swimming, but I keep circling back to the same cluster: the ones who put him there in the first place. LBJ and Westmoreland and Congress and the military-industrial complex and the American people who don't bother to connect the dots before coloring them in on their ballots, or who act thoughtlessly and squash the voices we need. God, this country could use healthy doses of Robert and Martin. Maybe with them, there's no Paul pitching kernels or any of the other sad, sorry shit I've seen. Maybe the kid's still back in Wisconsin milking cows instead of caving in skulls."

Tyler clutched his mug, his knuckles rigid, his fingers a mottle of white and crimson, and he drew long, slow breaths, as though trying to restrain something trying to snake out of him.

"I don't know," he said. "I just don't fucking know."

As Tyler's story unwound, I was calculating. I'd floated ROTC to my father as an option to get me to college sooner than later and postpone or even eliminate the possibility of my going to Vietnam. I knew the length of the contract after graduating. I also knew that Tyler's appearance didn't meet regulations for an officer in the United States Army. When he loosened his grip on his mug, I tightened my grip on Meg's hand. "I know some questions shouldn't be asked, but aren't you still an officer in the United States Army?"

Tyler beamed. "Hot damn, son. You know your poets and can do some math. Young lady," he said to Meg, "don't let this one get away." He shook his head and laughed, a low chuckle from his stomach. "When they shipped me stateside, I'm going through all that philosophical reckoning, and you'll like this one: I re-membered what Emerson said about scholars, how they're just pissing in a bucket unless they do something with their learn-ing, so I did something. I walked away, figured I could handle being AWOL. Let the powers-that-be expend their resources on keeping Ali locked up; I had some rope-a-dope of my own to steer clear of the authorities. 'Float like a butterfly,' as the champ says. I figured on Canada, but first I wanted to check on Paul—thought maybe I'd find him back here in Wisconsin, taking care of cows or something. That'd be an image I can live with, not the one I've been humping all this time. Along the way, I've been whooping it up at marches like our little soiree today. I blend in well enough not to draw any undue attention."

It was my turn to chuckle. "The panhandle philosopher," I said. My own laughter led me to release Meg's hand and realize just how tense I'd become sitting hunched at that table for so long. I raised my arms, pointing my elbows to either side, and stretched through my chest and back. Meg tilted her head and looked at me. "So does it do any good?" I asked Tyler, returning Meg's gaze. "Our marching, our chanting, our signs? Will it end it?"

"Damned if I know," he said. "I remember an old preacher saying 'the path to hell is paved with good intentions.' Hell, most of the peaceniks don't know Diem from their own asses if you press them on it." He paused. "I guess it doesn't hurt, though. If nothing else, venting like this might keep people from resorting to more extreme measures. They can talk all they want about bombing armories and 'by any means necessary,' but I find gatherings like this far more productive. Therapeutic, almost. Aristotle nailed it, you know. Everyone has stories to tell, things to vent. Something about tragedy and crowds and catharsis."

Tyler's words hung between us as streetlamps winked on outside the window.

When Meg and I left the Sunroom Café and parted ways with Tyler, we held each other tight as we walked back to campus and her dorm. She didn't speak, and I didn't press her to, though I could feel her processing a thousand things at once. When we entered her room, she still didn't speak; instead, she quickly undressed, and before I'd even removed my coat, she began undressing me—not violently, but urgently, unlike anything I'd felt coming from her. As we made love, that same urgency was there, in the strength of her arms, the placement of her hands, in the movement of her hips and her mouth. The silence was thick in the room as we lay in her bed.

Much later, our legs entwined, she finally spoke, her voice a mixture of regret and thankfulness. "That could've been..." she said. The unexpressed thought spoke with greater volume than it would have possessed had she voiced it. "He scared the hell out of me, Walt." She swallowed hard. "He's not much older than us, but he felt...I don't know, ancient? And the more he spoke, the more I kept asking, 'Could this have been you? Would this have been you?' I just couldn't stop those thoughts. They kept coming, that whole time. I'd nearly made you..."

"No," I whispered. "No, you didn't."

We both reached for the other's hand beneath the sheet as Meg continued. "And I kept telling myself that no, you wouldn't have, you know? But that 'what if?' just wouldn't go away. I couldn't shake it. And if you'd come home talking like that, carrying all that weight—how much of that would have been on me? How much of that would I have been responsible for?" She sniffed and wiped her eye with her free hand. "I'd held out hope—and I believe you did, too—that not only would you make it back alive, but that you'd make it back...okay. I encouraged that, Walt. Me. What if I'd buried you and all our dreams in some fool's hope, some pipe dream?" Her breathing grew more rapid and she turned onto her side to face me, her mouth inches away from me as she spoke, her voice now a desperate whisper that couldn't mask her sorrow. "I mean, I knew that terrible things happen over there. I saw it every day on the news and in the papers. I watched and read them just as much as you. But my god," she said, swallowing hard, "until you've spoken to someone who's actually been there, until you see that stare and hear that hollowness in his voice, until those words paint pictures no one should ever have to imagine, you can't even come close to feeling it, and—" Her words had sped up as she spoke, a rapid sibilance I felt as much as heard, but she paused and slowed down as she finished her thought. "And I don't know how I could've lived knowing I'd had a hand in that."

As we lay in her bed, I remembered the weight she'd helped me carry a year earlier and did my best to help Meg with her burden that April Fool's Day. "But I'm here," I said, "and you didn't. That's what matters now. That's all that matters. Your promise to me wouldn't have ruined me, Meg, and if things had gone differently, that promise would have brought me home. Brought me home. Me. Walt. Not Tyler or Paul or some other version of myself. Me. We're here. That's what matters. We're us."

We talked into the night before drifting off. At times the conversation was serious—the prospects of Tyler finding Paul and abandoning one life for another in Canada; of how Tyler couldn't be the only one affected by Vietnam as he was; of the ramifications of that war on soldiers, families, nations, on history itself—but more often than not, the conversation came back to us as we recounted stories of our past: of meeting in Tom's class, of past visits to the meadow and visits to come, of the time she spent with me and with my mother during my recuperation. And as we shared those stories, I sensed Meg's burden lighten. I felt it in her laughter, in the gravity of her gaze, in the very weight of her limbs and her touch as we lay beneath the sheets in the comfort of flesh on flesh as cold rain drummed against the window. I felt Meg's breath on my chest. "So it's okay?" she said, though it was more statement than question.

"Of course," I said. "Bum knee and all, everything is going to be okay."

"Good," she said as she yawned and exhaled, her breath tracing a warm path across my skin as she fell asleep.

"Good," I said. Her head rose and fell with my breathing, and her hair spilled over me onto the bed. I was thankful that Meg had found the peace we both needed. Good stories could do that.

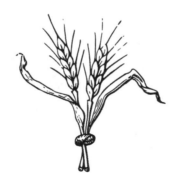

May 26, 1969

FOR THE FIRST time in years, I watched the Memorial Day parade from the sidewalk. Other than the perspective, little had changed about the event in the year that had passed since I last marched in it—the same atmosphere, the same groups and floats in the parade, the same crisp white shirts and blue pants and hats for my father and the other members of the VFW honor guard. I did note two changes, though. The honor guard's numbers had decreased, the result of two of its oldest members having died in the past year, and in the sea of crisp haircuts and heartland attire lining the sidewalks, I noticed one parade-goer who stood out from the rest, the one my father and the VFW had tried to recruit to their ranks but who'd declined the invitation in no uncertain terms: Elmer Baumgartner, who'd graduated my sophomore year and had gone on to do a tour in Vietnam before coming home to work at Owen's Fine Foods.

Elmer watched the parade while straddling his motorcycle, a Triumph TR5 Trophy, at the intersection of Main and Lake Streets. His smirk bore equal measures of Brando and James Dean, and he wore ripped jeans and an army shirt with the sleeves cut off, leaving ragged fringes whose long, trailing threads moved in the breeze. His last name was stenciled on a patch sewn just above his heart. When the back row of the marching band passed his post, Elmer started the Triumph, and as the VFW Honor Guard approached, he revved the motor to drown my father's commands beneath the rumble and whine of the Triumph. The Honor Guard passed Elmer, who tore into the street. He left a black streak on the pavement and wove between the final units in the parade as though they were markers on a slalom course. A horse reared, nearly throwing its rider, who lost his *Gunsmoke*-inspired Stetson as it fell atop a mound of horse apples the wheelbarrow crew hadn't yet scooped. An antique Farmall tractor backfired, its percussive report loud enough to compete with Elmer's Triumph for sonic supremacy in the wake of the band and Honor Guard. Meg, who was standing next to me, jumped, and I winced at the sound of the tractor and instinctively turned, placing myself between Meg and the street. The parade-watchers around us were also surprised—some throwing up their arms or putting their outstretched hands before their faces—and many expressed their disapproval: "that damn punk," "How dare he?" and "hardly surprising from one of *them*."

"All okay?" I asked Meg.

"Just peachy," she said, smoothing her dress. "That'll set some tongues to flapping."

She was right. In the year since honoring the first of Gillett's sons lost to Vietnam at the memorial marker, the handful of newly minted veterans who'd returned home found themselves the subject of gossip and criticism for not having fitted themselves neatly into the quilt of life in America's Dairyland. No one expressed such judgments to their faces—my hometown was too polite for that—but they had to have known, to have read it in people's eyes or heard it in the silence when they sat down at the counter in OJ's or walked down the aisles of the Ben Franklin.

"No doubt," I said, wishing on the one hand that I could convince everyone who was now disparaging Elmer to simply give him the time of day and listen without judgment to whatever he might or might not have to say, to let him know that he was truly home and that his membership in our community wasn't contingent upon subscribing a worldview that had struggled to accept the Beatles' mop tops, much less native sons who refused to march with the VFW.

"Tyler?" Meg asked.

I nodded.

"Do you think Elmer's spoken with anyone since coming home?" Meg asked.

"I don't know. I have my doubts," I said. "That's not to say that no one tried speaking to him." I could only imagine what had transpired when my father had met with Elmer and two other town sons to invite them to join the VFW and march with the honor guard in the parade. "I question, though, whether those people were willing or able to listen."

Meg and I walked to the memorial service three blocks down from where the St. John's Lutheran Church clock tower loomed over the end of Main Street. Again, few changes—the same benediction was delivered by Rev. Stubenvoll; the same remarks were delivered by the mayor; new plaques naming the fallen were revealed on the granite marker; a 21-gun salute was delivered under my father's command, though for some reason his voice lacked its customary resonance; and "Taps" was played by Meg's successor as first-chair trumpet in the band. Some of the same sensations I'd felt a year earlier came back, especially the feeling of oppressive weight. The source, however, was different, as I viewed the attendees through new lenses, lenses I now realized had been prescribed by the swirl of insanity in the world around me, ground by the rigor Tom's instruction and inspiration, and fitted by Tyler over an April Fool's Day meal in Madison.

Through those lenses, I watched those who lingered after the end of the service: sisters and mothers tracing the names on the markers, fathers and brothers standing with shoulders slouched and hands shoved into their pockets, veterans of World War II (my father among them) and Korea who looked at one another knowingly and spoke in low tones, making it impossible for me to hear what passed between them. As I watched them, I wondered about their stories, and the stories of those whose names were memorialized on the marker. I wondered if stories needing to be told had been told, if stories needing to be heard had been heard. I wondered if any of those accounts kept their tellers—or their listeners—up late at night. And I wondered if any of those stories, after telling, needed to be told and re-told, details added or deleted or adjusted to capture precisely what the stomach needed to feel.

Part of me felt drawn to approach those persons remaining at the memorial, to do whatever I must to encourage them to speak and convey that I would not only listen, but hear what they had to say. Watching them, though, my feet again felt as though they'd been encased in concrete. Whether that concrete had been poured by my own feelings of inadequacy or presumptuousness I couldn't say, but between that feeling and the other draw tugging at me—Meg's and my plans for a picnic at the meadow to celebrate an anniversary all our own—I couldn't bring myself to speak to any of them. My father mopped his brow and spoke with Herman Kirsch as Elmer Baumgartner sped past on his Triumph, his left arm raised and his middle finger extended. I promised to find a way of bringing those stories into the light of day.

Elmer's couldn't be the only ones.

Unlike our picnic the year before, Meg and I didn't find a profusion of daisies filling the meadow that day. The stalks were still there, rising from the grasses lanky and green with a few buds beginning to swell but still a week or more away from bursting. We also knew that we'd need to wrap up our picnic earlier than we'd like, as Clay, a newly minted graduate of Gillett High School, had been granted leave of all chores that holiday weekend and I was expected back on the farm for afternoon chores and milking.

We sat on our blanket near the base of the beech tree, over the exposed roots that had worn smooth from our many visits. Meg had prepared the same meal, and though neither of us had gifts to give that day, we recollected the presents we'd exchanged a year earlier. She wore hers as she did every day, the agate no less vibrant as it dangled from the silver chain and rested against her breastbone.

We'd been together since early in our junior year of high school, but the meadow hadn't lost its luster; it was a privileged place, our most special place—the spot that had first drawn us together, the spot where we'd first kissed, first made love, first dreamed together, still dreamed together. Those dreams now, however, weren't haunted by specters. I was, and would remain, stateside. We'd both been successful in our first taste of college. We'd made each other promises and hadn't abandoned them. We shared a history and a future, and as Meg put it, "we still like each other after all this time, so that works out."

We'd finished our meal beneath the tree at the edge of the meadow and were discussing ways to carve out more time together that summer given schedules that found both of us working jobs to make money for school when we heard the siren, a distant rise and fall carrying over farm fields and riding the wind until it reached us. We didn't hear it for long, perhaps 30 seconds, perhaps a minute, but in that time the siren's volume had grown louder. And when the siren stopped, when whatever emergency vehicle had reached its destination, it stopped to our south and west. For a moment, it seemed that the siren had ceased at the farm, but just as quickly, I told myself it could just as easily have been at the Zwijacz or Lauersdorf farms, or even at Art Motzer's or Wally Mueller's homes. Sound played weird tricks when traveling over long distances.

I checked my watch. It was 3 o'clock, and I suggested we pack our things. We'd made the walk that day from the farm, and it would take us some time to walk back. "Can't make the old man upset," I told Meg.

"Or the girlfriend," she joked and kissed me. Strawberries and lemonade. "We'll just let that simmer," she said.

We walked through the meadow, the grasses and daisy stems brushing against our legs, to the short path that led to the railroad tracks, which we took to the eastern edge of my family's property. There, we took another short path through the stand of trees that buffered the railroad from a hay field. The alfalfa had grown just past knee-high and was a particularly rich green that year. Faint purple buds had just begun to appear, and I knew that my father would start cutting the first crop harvest within a few days.

Meg and I hugged the edge of the field as we walked, and when we reached the top of a gentle swell where my deer stand leaned against a high cedar, the farm came into view.

That's when my heart fell.

Almost a mile away, the lights of an ambulance flashed in front of my family's home. The sound of its doors slamming shut reached us, and I dropped everything.

I looked at Meg.

The siren sounded again, wailing with a timbre bordering on human.

"Go," she said, and I ran through the field toward home.

My father died at 10 pm.

He'd suffered the first heart attack shortly after 2:30, prompting my mother to call the ambulance, and the fatal attack came later that night. My mother had gone to the hospital with him in the ambulance, and Clay arrived after being tracked down at the Memorial Day town picnic on Main Street. My mother's call from the hospital shortly after the ambulance had arrived was fragmented, and her words came to me in fits and starts. In her voice, I could hear her efforts to remain calm, could hear the pauses and irregular breathing that demonstrated her inability to entirely comport herself. She told me to stay home for now, to do the chores and milk the cows before coming to the hospital myself—that my father "was resting comfortably," and that the doctors were "keeping an eye on him."

Meg insisted on staying with me to help with the work. She called her parents to tell them what had happened and changed into some of my work clothes, which hung from her slim frame and required the strategic use of a belt. She worked without reservation or hesitation. She herded cows from the pasture. She hauled bales of hay to the heifers' feeder outside the basement loafing barn. She milked cows for the first time that night and had no problem toting and lifting surge buckets to the aluminum milk cans and pouring milk through the filtered funnel. And as we worked together, she helped me to remain calm with a touch, a word, a glance. She was my antidote to the fear and dread that threatened me just as I'd sensed it threatening my mother.

When we'd finished the work and returned the cows to pasture for the night, we went into the house and cleaned up. Meg drove us to the hospital, where my mother fell into my arms and began to cry and cry, loudly at first, but then just shivers. Her tears soaked through my shirt, but I didn't mind. If I could bring her any degree of comfort, I would. I'd seen her change in the past year. She'd definitely aged: her hair, once a brown so deep it was almost black, had grown salt-and-pepper; wrinkles had etched themselves more deeply into the geology of her face; and more and more often, not just at a moment of distress in the family waiting room of the ICU of the Shawano Memorial Hospital, she seemed tired, and not just physically. In the two weeks since returning from Madison, I'd noticed that though she still performed the same tasks of home, farm, and garden she'd always performed, they now lacked the vitality I'd grown accustomed to witnessing in her. She even spoke less, and when she did speak, her words articulated the same optimistic outlook as ever, but I didn't sense that her heart was fully invested in them.

Clay moved soundlessly across the waiting room, as though stalking something only he saw. Unlike my mother over the past two weeks, Clay had seemed ecstatic. He was thrilled to graduate and to have seen the inside of a classroom for the last time. Not that my brother was unintelligent; he simply saw little use for formal education and was perfectly content seated at the pinnacle of the bell curve. His final season of high school ball had been stellar, and he frustrated scout after scout by rebuffing their advances in favor of his real goal: becoming part of the 101st Airborne, "a real Screaming Eagle," as he put it. Many of those scouts had tried to reason with my father, hoping that he might sway my brother to accept the signing bonuses that would be offered him as a high pick in the amateur draft and suggesting a host of methods to keep Clay from being obliged to active duty. My father proudly reminded them that Clay wasn't afraid to serve, that he was freely choosing to enlist in the army and that he embodied what "too many of those long-haired hippy types" lacked: a genuine sense of duty. I thought Clay was an idiot, but I remembered my talks with Tom; not wanting to create choppy seas for us or for my family in the time before Clay reported to Basic and I returned to school, I opted to remain silent.

I could see my father from the waiting area in the ICU. His bed, blocked off from others in the unit by portable curtains on either side, was directly across from the waiting area door. I stood at the door, looking through the doubled-glass pane encasing a network of fine wires in a diamond pattern. He was unconscious, his skin ashen in the low light, and a host of wires and tubes linked him to beeping monitors and bags of fluids.

Shortly after 9 o'clock, a doctor came to consult our family. He said that in addition to the heart attack, he also believed my father had suffered a stroke, but that he wouldn't know for certain unless my father regained consciousness. He told us that he could make no promises, that we should hope for the best but prepare for the worst.

The hospital chaplain had already come to speak with us, and shortly after the doctor left, Rev. Stubenvoll came to see us. After getting the basics of what had happened and my father's condition, he suggested we go to my father's bed, where he asked if he might share a passage with us. Rev. Stubenvoll, he of thundering fire and brimstone sermons and theology drawn from Luther himself, opened his worn, leather-bound Bible and quietly read a passage from Paul's Letter to the Ephesians: *And you were dead in the trespasses and sins in which you once walked, following the course of this world, following the prince of the power of the air, the spirit that is now at work in the sons of disobedience—among whom we all once lived in the passions of our flesh, carrying out the desires of the body and the mind, and were by nature children of wrath, like the rest of mankind. But God, being rich in mercy, because of the great love with which he loved us, even when we were dead in our trespasses, made us alive together with Christ—by grace you have been saved—and raised us up with him and seated us with him in the heavenly places in Christ Jesus, so that in the coming ages he might show the immeasurable riches of his grace in kindness toward us in Christ Jesus. For by grace you have been saved through faith. And this is not your own doing; it is the gift of God, not a result of works, so that no one may boast. For we are his workmanship, created in Christ Jesus for good works, which God prepared beforehand, that we should walk in them.*

At the time, as Rev. Stubenvoll read those words, I was numb to them. I assumed he'd selected them with purpose, intended them to have meaning not only for my father but for all of us, but as much as I tried to focus on them, all I could conjure were images of my father that starkly contrasted the one now before me. I pictured him in his hunting clothes, his rifle slung over his shoulder, tromping off to the woods. I pictured him in the crisp uniform of the VFW, marching in parades down Main Street. I pictured him in the portrait my mother kept on her dresser, a formal shot of him in his army dress uniform before being sent to Europe—his face young and smooth, free of wrinkles, not at all unlike Clay's or mine; his haircut high and tight; his eyes full of confidence, duty, and commitment. I also pictured our arguments, his brow furrowed and eyes narrowed, tendons sticking out from his neck as his face flushed a deeper and deeper shade of crimson, repeating the platitudes he could never make hit their mark with me as they did with my brother.

I'd have liked a platitude or two at that moment, would have welcomed his face turning crimson, but he lay there, the hiss of the respirator and the faint *beep* of the EKG drowning out whatever Rev. Stubenvoll was saying as he led us in the Lord's Prayer. With the amen, he offered final handshakes and left, insisting that we call if he was needed and telling us he would visit again in the morning.

The three of us remained bedside. I felt odd, as though my head was tethered, floating well above the rest of me. My mother looked drained, her skin nearly as pale as my father's, as she reached over the railing to hold his hand. Clay surprised me with his willingness to speak, not only to our mother and me, but to our father. "He's going to make it, see? He's a fighter. It's what Neumanns are. You're going to make it, Dad. You will."

After several minutes, our mother sent Clay and me away, telling us she needed a minute alone with him. We returned to the waiting room, where Clay turned on the television to an episode of "Laugh-In" and turned down the volume completely. Goldie Hawn gyrated on the screen. I shook my head and sat down, watching my mother through the window as she bent over the bed to speak to my father, her form a silhouette backlit by the monitors at the head of the bed. As she spoke, I saw her jerk upright and turn toward the nurse's station, calling out the single word "help!" that carried through the wood and glass of the waiting room door, prompting Clay and me to rush toward the bed. Nurses converged, closely followed by the attending physician, and we were all ushered away, relegated to the waiting room, its door now attended by hospital security. I watched what I could through the window as the doctor and nurses dropped the bed's rails and worked on my father. I don't know how long they worked on him; it may have been a minute, five minutes, even longer. I had no sense of time's passage. Finally, I saw the doctor drop his hands and let himself go limp as he spoke to one of the nurses before approaching the waiting room door. My mother turned to me and I encircled her with my arms, her mouth open but no sound coming out.

I held her close, astonished at how slight she'd become.

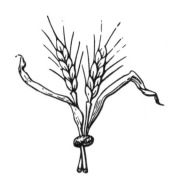

May 27 – July 1, 1969

I STAYED AT the hospital with my mother and Clay until Aunt Kay, my mother's youngest sister, arrived. We decided that someone needed to go home for a few hours of sleep before the morning chores and milking. I volunteered for duty. After she'd taken care of formalities at the hospital, Clay would bring our mother to our aunt's house and stay there with her. Meg drove me home, and I drifted off in the car on the way back to Gillett. Thank God for her. When I'd left the ICU, she was still there, waiting. She'd known as soon as she'd seen me, and we held each other beneath a long light fixture's harsh fluorescent glow. "I'm so sorry, Walt," she said. Her words had been the first thing to pierce the numbness that had engulfed me since we'd seen the flashing lights of the ambulance from the hayfield. In Meg's arms, I finally allowed myself to cry.

By the time she brought me home, I was exhausted. She asked if I'd like her to stay with me, and I told her I would. I wasn't a great conversationalist at that point, but Meg didn't mind. I drank a glass of water and brushed my teeth before going up to my bedroom. Meg came with me. I set my alarm clock for 5:30, undressed, and crawled beneath the covers. She sat on the bed and stroked my head, her touch both strong and gentle, soothing me in the way she moved over my scalp and brushed my cheek. She didn't speak; she just stayed there with me, keeping a silent vigil as I drifted off to sleep, and she was there in the morning when I awoke, ready to help with the tasks the morning would bring.

The next two weeks were a blur. Hotdishes and pans of bars began arriving at our home from friends and neighbors the day after my father's death. Visitation took place at Kuehl Funeral Home Wednesday, and the funeral was Thursday. Rev. Stubenvoll extolled my father's devotion to family, farm, and country in a eulogy built around the Gospel story of Jesus raising Lazarus from the dead. It was one of the more impressive bits of preaching I'd heard him deliver, as he pulled out the nature of faith and belief as embodied in the passage and connected it to what my father had done in nurturing farm and family and in having served his country with such pride, using that trifecta as evidence of my father's faith in God's word. Interment in the church cemetery immediately followed the service and included an Army Honor Guard which offered a

21-gun salute and folded thirteen times the flag that had draped my father's casket before presenting it to my mother. A meal was prepared by the ladies' auxiliary of our church and served in the basement fellowship hall.

Having family there helped—my aunts, uncles, and cousins being there, offering their condolences and kind thoughts provided a measure of comfort for me, and especially for my mother. My greatest comfort, though, came in having both Meg and Tom there. Meg and her parents sat three pews behind my family in church, and from the time the service ended, Meg was at my side. Tom being there was a genuine surprise. He'd been planning to return to Chicago to visit his mother now that the school year had ended, but he told me that Meg's father had contacted him with the news and that he'd decided to postpone that trip because he "wanted to be of help in any way he could." I thought I'd cried myself out earlier, but Meg's and Tom's presence after the service, both at the cemetery and in the fellowship hall for the meal prepared by the St. John's Ladies Auxiliary, tapped a new well. Their presence spoke volumes, and I couldn't find the words to convey my gratitude.

I was supposed to have begun a summer job with Wagner Gas & Electric the day after Memorial Day, but that was out of the question. Instead, I took my father's place in the seat of the larger of our two tractors and began cutting swaths of the year's first crop of alfalfa. Both Tom and Meg came to the farm daily, helping to perform the routine tasks so that Clay and I could focus on cutting the hay and then chopping it into the boxes that fed it into the hopper of the blower that sent it sixty feet up to drop into the concrete silo. Clay and I alternated between chopping the cut hay in the fields and bringing the boxes back to the farm. Our mother made certain everyone was well-fed, and I didn't let a day pass without thanking Meg and Tom for the help they provided.

When the first crop of hay had been harvested, Tom returned to Chicago to visit his mother, and Meg and I spent as much time as we could in the meadow, where the daisies were now in full bloom. My mother decided that given the paths Clay and I had chosen for ourselves, she would sell the livestock and equipment, that it wouldn't be fair to expect either of us to one day take over an operation that wasn't in our hearts. It had been one of those "what if" conversations she and my father had had prior to his death. She would keep the land and rent it to our neighbor, Melvin Zwijacz, whose son Robert had been wanting to expand the size of their herd. He and my parents had helped each other over the years, and my mother felt that's what my father would have wanted—to do right by a good neighbor while ensuring some income for my mother.

I was happy about her decision to keep the land for other reasons. My grandparents had homesteaded the farm; it had brought them to America from Germany so many years before. I'd walked each acre with my grandmother more times than I could count. The *herrlichkeit* had fed our family and herd as much as the tillable acreage and far more than the stands of forest or low-lying wetlands my father loved to hunt; for that land to pass outside our family would have thrown some essential component of the cosmic order out of balance.

Those days must have been difficult for my mother. I'd witnessed, for nearly twenty years, the love she felt for my father in the face of his imperfections and the fact that he was capable of frustrating her far more than she ever let on, so for him to so suddenly be gone had to have sent her reeling. In addition to the loss, she now had to take care of settling the estate, preparing for the auction—scheduled for July 5, the same day Clay was scheduled to leave for Basic—and taking care of my father's personal effects.

Some of those decisions were fairly easy. His clothes went to charity. Clay loved hunting far more than I did, so our father's hunting equipment went to him. My father had been in band when he was in school, so I was given his old trumpet. He'd also kept on his nightstand the Bible that had belonged to his mother before she'd died. Given my closeness to her, I was also given that Bible.

The final item my mother went through was the old, padlocked footlocker he kept tucked away in an upstairs room where we kept winter coats and hunting gear. Packed inside the foot locker were pieces of the life he'd lived during his service in the Army during World War II: written commendations from his commanding officers; boxed medals, decorations, and service ribbons, including marksmanship medals and a purple heart; several pieces of clothing, ranging from fatigues to a full-dress uniform; a shoebox of letters he'd received from my mother while he was away from home; the dog tags he'd worn the first morning he'd come to see me in the hospital; and snapshots of a much younger version of my father than I'd ever known.

In some, he was wearing the same dress uniform stored in the footlocker, standing in what appeared to be a ballroom amidst other young men just like him. In others, he simply wore a t-shirt and cargo pants and was seated with other soldiers, each of them raising a bottle of beer.

The last items she removed from the footlocker were two envelopes. On the front of one was Clay's name, and on the front of the other was mine. "Your father very much wanted each of you to have these once he'd passed on," she said, "though both of us had hoped you wouldn't be receiving these for many, many years." She paused before continuing, as though she were trying out what she'd say before the words passed her lips. "I'm pretty certain I know what he's written in the letters. Most of it, at least." She sat at the end of the bed, looking down at her hands folded in her lap. She didn't look up at either of us when she spoke. "If you want to...I'd be more than happy to talk to... to talk with you. After you've read what your father has written." The formal shot of my father in uniform gazed back from my mother's nightstand, and she looked up, joining that image of him in staring back at us.

I was baffled. Though we often disagreed, I knew that my father was an intelligent man. He read often, and sometimes, when I wasn't frustrated to the point of wanting to disown him, I thought of him with a certain degree of pride as the farmer Crevecoeur had in mind when he wrote of the American who nurtured the fields through the labor of his hands by day and nurtured his mind through the labor of his intellect by night.

The envelope felt strange in my hands, at once hot and cold

between my fingertips. Part of me was compelled to open it immediately, there in my parents' bedroom, and read it in front of my mother, but that wouldn't have been right. She may have known the letter's contents, but my father had intended them for me. And though we'd arrived at an uneasy peace between us in the months following my injury, we'd never formally declared a truce; ours was amity tinged by uncertainty. If he wanted that letter to be for me, that is how I would receive it. Alone with him, the final sit down the two of us could never bring ourselves to share.

I went to the telephone hanging from the wall next to the front door and called Meg. She'd thought it would be fun for us to listen to the Beatles' *White Album* that evening and was expecting me to come see her. It would be something to take our minds off the events of the last couple of weeks. I told her about the letter and that I would still come to her house, but that I needed to read it first.

"You could always bring it along and read it here," she said.

I was tempted by her offer; her voice sounded so good in the earpiece.

I shook my head. "No," I said, "I owe him this. We can talk about it later."

"I understand," she said. "You always know where to find me."

She was right.

I went to my bedroom, closed the door, and sat down at the old teacher's desk I'd rescued from the high school when the district had replaced them with newer models. I held the envelope on either end and studied my name as my father had written it in pencil. His script was rounder and more upright than mine, and the lines of the letters at times appeared as though his hand had trembled when he wrote. I took a deep breath, slipped my index finger beneath the flap, and slid it the length of the envelope. The five pages on which the letter had been written were folded in upon themselves twice, and the top of the first page bore the date he'd written it: July 6, 1968. I began reading.

My father didn't write artfully, but he did write clearly and effectively. The first two pages didn't take long to strike a chord. He stated his love for me and acknowledged that he'd had, and was having, difficulty reconciling with the fact that the person I am wasn't entirely the person he imagined I'd be when he and my mother had discovered she was pregnant. Despite that, he was "proud of me" and "regretted not doing a better job of showing it." My eyes stung, in a good way, as I read these sentiments from my father—the stiffest upper lip in the Midwest actually did recognize me on some level for who I was and what I was about. My emotions changed, though, when the tone and drift of the letter, and even the script in which it was written, underwent a change on the third page. That's when he began writing about his life in the military, about the things I'd pressed him to share but which had prompted him to either leave the room or to retreat within himself.

That's when he revealed truth.

I'd only known—because he'd only shared—the basics. Army. World War II. Tour of duty in Europe. In the letter he expanded upon that. He'd been a member of the 18th Infantry Regiment, 1st

Infantry Division, 1ˢᵗ Battalion—a battalion that had helped take Normandy but had suffered light casualties because they'd landed thirty minutes late due to the congestion offshore. *I thanked God that day for that circumstance. It probably saved my life,* my father wrote, *but I cursed him too. The waste I saw on that beach was beyond description. I've known many ministers to be colorful from the pulpit in their descriptions of hell, but if that's what hell is, it's a walk in the park compared to what we waded into that day. I won't even try to describe just what I saw. I don't have your way with words, but I can only ask you to trust me. It wasn't pretty.*

I paused to reach for a tissue and blot my eyes. I was growing angry with my father for having kept those things bottled up for so many years, but that anger was tempered by empathy, thanks to Tyler and the epiphany of April Fool's Day. I continued reading. *I must try to describe for you one image from that day, though. As we crossed the beach and began charging uphill, my friend Wyatt stayed close to me. He was a good person. He was from Minnesota, from a farm, like me, and we'd been together since Basic Training. He had the brightest blue eyes I'd ever seen. Given our similar backgrounds, we understood each other well, and we grew close. It helped, having someone to talk to. He was like a brother. We joked about someday owning farms next to each other, helping each other out. We'd even share equipment, buy the biggest grain thresher we could find and do twice the work in half the time. It helped remind me of home and what your mother and I would create together. I loved that. I loved him for that. As Wyatt and I moved up the hill, he took a round to the chest. I can still remember the sound of it striking him, the crunching and the wetness of it. I remember screaming, but I can't remember hearing myself as I watched. The impact threw his arms forward as the rest of him was thrown backwards. I called for a medic, but no one came. It wouldn't have done any good regardless. I knelt by him and held his hand. I didn't know if he even knew I was there until his head rolled to my side and he looked at me. "Otto," he said, "think of me some day when it's a good harvest." I told him I would do that. He said, "Good," then he smiled a little and blew out his last breath. And that's the image I carried with me from Normandy. Wyatt lying there, his head toward the beach and those blue eyes of his totally empty of life. I lowered the lids and remained at his side until common sense kicked in and I realized I was nothing more than a sitting duck.*

I wished my father had told me that story much, much earlier. I wished that I'd been able to listen to him, that perhaps his being able to share it with me would have brought him some degree of comfort and would have helped me to understand him better—not agree with him or his wishes for my future, but to understand him in a way I never had when he was alive. I could tell from the letter that writing about Wyatt and Normandy couldn't have been easy, that he'd still carried baggage almost a quarter-century later as he finally shared with me. At that moment, I felt the anger I'd once harbored for him slipping away. At that moment, I was willing to let go of things.

I continued reading. He went on to tell how the 1st Battalion had later that year been charged with taking Hill 239, Crucifix Hill, just outside the German village Haaren. My father was a member of a pillbox assault team, and as he wrote about that day in October 1944, he continued writing in the straightforward, plain-spoken manner he'd written the letter to that point, but the letter's contents nonetheless reminded me of Tyler; I could sense in my father's words much of what I'd sensed from him—the fear, the blinding confusion, the abandonment of fighting for country as death and fire from both sides of the conflict rained down around him. For my father that day, the mission was no longer taking Hill 239; instead, it was survival.

He had been part of the second wave, following the leading rifle platoon that had stormed Crucifix Hill with flamethrowers, Banaglore torpedoes, and detonation charges. *Our task was slow and deadly,* he wrote. *We had support from a battery of M3's, but those pillboxes were thick. We fixed bayonets for a reason. It was just as ugly as Normandy. The death and destruction may not have been on that scale, but man-made death in any form is not a beautiful thing. A reasonable path eventually opened. I fired often as I charged up the hill. I don't know if the shots hit their target, and to be honest, I often didn't know what the target was. But I did make it to the top of the hill, where a large wooden cross rose from the ground. There at the foot of the cross was a wounded German soldier. I raised my rifle and aimed at him. He'd already lost part of his arm, and his leg was bent in a way it wasn't meant to bend. With the one whole arm he still had, he raised his hand and spread his fingers wide. His eyes showed no anger, just fear and pleading. They were a bright blue. He called to me, "Bitte hilf mir. Barmherzigkeit." I remembered enough German being spoken by your grandparents to know what he was saying. "Please help me. Show mercy." None of it mattered.*

Before I could think, I ran at him with my rifle lowered, and I stabbed him with my bayonet. I felt the crunch of bones, both as the blade entered him and as I tried to remove it from his chest. I had to place my foot on his sternum to remove the blade.

That German soldier is the other image I carry with me from my time in the Army. Both visit me sometimes. Usually, it is when I'm on a tractor late at night. In the spring, when I am working the fields for planting, or in the fall, when I am chopping third crop hay. There is something about the rumble of machines and the repetition of motion that brings them to me. Other times, they come to me in silence, like when I'm sitting in my deer stand and the sunlight coming through the naked branches has the same quality as the sunlight on each of those days. Sometimes they come to me when I'm lying in bed and can't sleep. I try speaking to them when they visit. I try to send them words through force of will and mental energy, but I never succeed. Wyatt remains lifeless and the German soldier continues to plead with me. I fail just as miserably with spirits and memory as I failed in Europe.

He'd shared more with me in a few pages than he had in my nearly twenty years. He'd shown a humanity I'd never witnessed in him, and he'd drawn an empathy from me that I never suspected I'd feel for my father. Guilt. Remorse. I'd never even imagined such an imposing figure in my world could have felt such emotions. I wish my father had ended his letter there. He didn't.

So that's one of the reasons I feel so strongly about you and your brother serving now. You can succeed where I failed. Or perhaps in your case, after that doctor said everything he said this morning, I should say that you wouldn't have failed. I tell myself that I've done all I could to make you and Clay into men who have the principles I must have lacked in some fashion. In the big picture, you would have made right a terrible wrong I committed on Crucifix Hill in October 1944.

I like to think that I serve as a role model for the two of you. I tell myself that one day, when I am no longer here, you and your brother will live lives and have families of your own that can draw in some way upon the example I've tried to set for you. I give my everything to this farm to cultivate good crops and manage a good herd. I do all I can to provide for you and Clay and your mother and to give you comfortable lives. I've tried to teach you the importance of hard work, and I've also tried to give you the opportunities to do things that make you happy. I'm faithful to God, and I try to instill in you a love of America that we all must share if this country isn't to split at its seams. I like to think I'm a good man, but you and your brother can be even better men. That is where I can give myself no margin for error. You must be a better man than I am.

Even after such terrible failure on my part, I received the blessings of this great nation. Your mother and I would not have been able to buy the farm from my parents without the loan I received through the G.I. Bill. I had committed terrible wrongs. I hadn't been able to save my friend. I murdered a German soldier begging for mercy and compassion. I did all that was asked of me, yet I failed. This nation has given me the means to build a life and provide for my family. It fed my hopes and dreams when I had no right to ask for even a scrap from the table. I've long since paid back that government loan for the farm, but I still carry a far larger debt. That debt is one I can only repay through the devoted service of my sons, who I have raised to be better than me. You and Clay can't be weak like me.

The son of a bitch. I swept the pages from my desk and brought my fist down upon its surface, then stormed out of my room. "How do you like that, Clay?" I shouted at his bedroom door as I stomped down the stairs. My mother was waiting at the kitchen table, and she rose from her seat when I entered the room. "You knew, didn't you?" I said.

"Walt, I tried—"

I didn't let her finish. "Well you didn't try hard enough." I heard her voice but couldn't make out her words through the door slamming behind me on my way to the car. I didn't know exactly what I wanted or how to find it at that moment. I just knew that I needed to leave, needed to find Meg, needed to gather my thoughts, and needed to come up with a plan.

I checked my watch in the glow of the dome light when I pulled into the Eiseths' driveway. 10:00. I normally wouldn't have dreamed of knocking on their door at that hour, but this was an exceptional circumstance. Mr. Eiseth answered the door. "We were wondering," he said, "if you might still come by. Meg was expecting you, but she said you'd called about a letter."

As always, his voice was rich and his demeanor calming, and Mr. Eiseth's simply talking to me took some of the edge off my tension. "That's right. We were going through the last of my father's things, and my mother gave my brother and me each a letter he'd written. I wanted some time to…read the letter."

"Understood, Walt. I believe Meg is out back." He led me to the gazebo he'd built, where Meg sat in a wicker rocker beneath a reading lamp. When she heard us approach, she stood up, came down the steps, and appeared to float across the yard toward us. "I'll leave you two alone," Mr. Eiseth said. He patted my shoulder and returned to the house.

Meg hugged me. It felt good to be held and to hold her, to feel her pressed against me, returning my embrace. "So much for the *White Album* tonight," I said.

"It's not going anywhere," she said, "and we have lots of days ahead." I felt some more of the tension in me melting. "Want to talk?" she asked.

I nodded, and she led me to the gazebo stairs, where a thick, soft blanket was draped over the railing. Meg removed it and spread it on the lawn beneath the span of a red maple's branches. We lay on our backs next to each other, looking at the sky dotted with stars. I fixed on the North Star as Meg took my hand and waited for me to speak.

I didn't speak right away. I focused on the strength of Meg's hand, the warmth of her arm against mine, the cushion of the lawn and the blanket beneath me, the damp night air filling my lungs as I breathed. I don't know how long we lay there in silence, and when I finally did speak, I didn't take my gaze away from the North Star. It was as if having something unmoving and permanent to hold in my vision allowed me to channel my thoughts more effectively. I told her everything from that night, the objects in the foot locker, the letters, my mother's preface to giving them to Clay and me. Then I began telling her about the letter itself, reading it at the desk in my room. Meg rode the roller coaster along with me. She knew as well as I did my feelings about my father, so as I told her about the first part of the letter, I could feel her smile in the way she held my hand. When I told her of his finally opening up about his time in the Army, I could feel the chill pass through her, the gooseflesh on her arms, and though she didn't want to interrupt me, I could hear her whispering to herself. After telling her about the letter, we sat up, and I told her of my reaction to it, of storming out of the house, of my mother, of driving here, to her, where I needed to be. And though I didn't want to ask it, I couldn't help myself: "What does it all mean, Meg?"

She'd been lightly scratching my back through my shirt, calming me, but when I asked her that question, she stopped and shifted to look me straight in the eye. "I wish I knew, Walt. I wish I had an answer." I looked down at her hands, stained by paint. "What are you feeling right now?"

I'd come down from the peak of rage I'd ascended earlier, but anger and resentment—a particularly bitter resentment—still sat in the pit of my stomach. We continued talking; actually, it was more me talking and Meg carefully asking me questions that allowed me to begin sifting through what I thought and felt. How could he have thought of me as the penance for his sin? Was what he had done on Crucifix Hill even a sin? Knowing what he knew, how could he wish upon his sons even a fraction of what awaited Clay and me on the path he envisioned us taking? After a time, we wore out such discussion—not that the conversation I'd begun with Meg was finished, but that we both needed something else. We spoke of our plans for the rest of the summer, of our hopes for the year ahead in Madison, of our dreams for the lifetime unfolding before us. And as we spoke, the night itself slipped away and the first signs of dawn appeared in the eastern sky. I knew I needed to return home, not only to do the morning milking and chores, but for other things as well.

I thanked Meg for being with me, for guiding me through the night, but a host of questions still gnawed at me. As I left, I tried to knit the lot of them into a single question I hoped Meg might be able to answer: "What do I do now?"

Meg smiled and as we faced each other, she held both of my hands in hers. "I think the answer to that one is fairly simple," she said. "Call Tom."

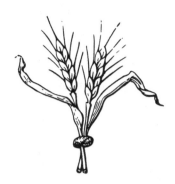

July 1, 1969

I CALLED TOM the next morning. I thanked him for having given me his mother's number in Chicago with the directive to call him if I needed anything, and I apologized for having taken him up on the offer. He told me not to sweat it, that he didn't make empty offers or promises. I shared the basics—my father had left a letter about his service experience and his hopes for me, that the letter had shaken me—but I wasn't about to unpack its full contents over the phone.

"Shaken?" Tom asked.

I felt my cheeks flare as I remembered reading the final paragraph and leaving the house the night before with my brother in his room and my mother in the kitchen. "That might be putting it mildly," I said.

"You're not one to exaggerate," he said. "I was headed back up to Gillett later today anyway. My Polish mother was curious about life outside the big city this Independence Day, so we're heading north for a taste of rural Americana. I'll call you when we're back in town. Let's get together. I'd like to hear more about this letter."

"I appreciate that," I said, and went off to my room to sleep. I needed to speak to my mother and Clay, but at that point, I was bone tired and knew I needed some rest.

My mother's knocking at my bedroom door awakened me. My eyes burned as I opened them and looked at my alarm clock. A blurry 2:30. My mouth was pasty. She knocked again. "Walt?"

My head felt thick. "Come in," I said, rolling toward the door.

She stepped in tentatively, as though her tread might cause some undue disturbance. "I just wanted to check on you."

"I'm fine," I said, sitting up in my bed and stretching.

"After last night—"

"I know," I said, "I need to talk to you about that."

"The way you ran off. I was worried. I figured you'd gone to the Eiseth's, and not long after you left, Meg's father called, so I knew you were alright. But still…"

"You knew," I said. "About Wyatt and Crucifix Hill and penance, didn't you?"

She didn't speak or look at me.

"How could you?" I demanded.

"What was I supposed to do? He wanted you to have the letter someday." she said, shrugging.

"Not that," I said, "I get that. What about that garbage about repaying debts through Clay and me?"

"Walt, you have to understand something. He was my husband—"

"And Clay and I are your sons, not penance for the sins of the father or some kind of twisted blood money."

"—and you and Clay are my sons. This is my family. This is my home." She was looking me in the eye now.

"Didn't it occur to you that I might have come back in a flag-draped coffin and that they'd be putting my name on that massive hunk of granite in town?"

"I'd be lying if I said it didn't," she said, her gray eyes flaring.

"Clay leaves in four days, Mom. We'll see him after Basic and AIT, but once he hops that plane, he may never come back."

"So what would you have done, Walt?" She set her chin firmly. "Put yourself in my shoes."

"Right is right, Mom." My father had fallen back on that line more than once.

"You don't even know," she said, shaking her head. "You don't even know."

Her voice wasn't like my father's or Clay's when we confronted one another. Instead of directing condescension at me, she directed it at herself. I also sensed sadness—profound sadness—that made me pause before I spoke again. "What don't I know, Mom? What haven't you told me?"

She clenched her jaw and sat down in the chair at my desk, drumming her fingers on the surface for a long, long time before she spoke. "You didn't see him once he came home," she said.

"He wasn't the same man I'd made promises to before he left." I'd known that my parents had met and were engaged before he'd gone overseas and that they married shortly after he returned in 1945, but beyond that, I knew precious few details of their early life together. "His love of country was always there," she said. "It came down from your grandmother. The *herrlichkeit*. Opportunity in the New World. Belief in limitless promise and possibility. That sort of faith was attractive. From the day we met at that dance, I could sense your father's capacity for commitment. That counted for something. It meant something to me," she said.

She went on to describe how they'd met in Shawano when they were both seniors in high school, how he'd been clear about his intentions to enlist after graduating and how, months after they'd begun dating and their high school graduations drew near, that enlistment would be so much easier with a promise from his one-and-only. She'd given him that promise, and he'd given her a ring, the same one she was wearing that day in my room. It felt odd, hearing about my parents dancing and dreaming and making promises not unlike those Meg and I had made; it cast them in a different light, humanized them in a way I had never allowed myself to experience and which they, my father in particular, never promoted. More than once, I'd pictured them at my age and tried to imagine them thinking what I thought, feeling what I felt, knowing they were capable of such thoughts and feelings, but until that afternoon with my mother, I'd never been able to move beyond intellectualizing it. When my mother shared their story, I felt it for the first time.

When my father returned from Europe and was discharged, she said he'd changed. She never questioned his commitment to her or to their future, but he didn't speak as much, didn't laugh as much. Even as they planned and prepared for their wedding, she sensed he was holding something back. She sometimes caught him staring into the distance, and sometimes he needed to spend time by himself. She tried to get him to talk about his experiences in the war, but he wouldn't, and when my grandparents expressed their pride for the decorations and recognition he'd received, he dismissed the attention.

It wasn't until after they were married and she awoke in the middle of the night to find my father's side of the bed empty that she compelled him to talk. She'd risen from bed and went to look for him. They'd already purchased the farm from my grandparents and were living in the only home I'd ever known. He wasn't in the kitchen or living room, and she saw no lights in the barn to indicate that he'd gone to check on a cow ready to freshen. She didn't find him until she went upstairs and looked out the door to the small porch jutting northward from the back of the house: he was curled against the railing, clutching his deer rifle.

"I was scared," she said, "and I wasn't about to disturb him. I went downstairs, but I didn't sleep a wink the rest of the night. He came back to our room just before the alarm went off to wake us for milking. He said little that morning. I didn't know if he'd seen me or not; he hadn't looked back, just stared off over the orchard toward the hill rising up just past our property line.

"At lunch, I confronted him. It wasn't the first time I'd tried getting him to talk, but I'd never forced the issue. 'I'm your wife,'

215

I said, 'and if I'm going to remain your wife, you're going to tell me why you were up there on the porch with your rifle last night.'"

I'd always known that my mother had a special kind of courage, but her having confronted my father like that confirmed it. My heart opened for her, and while the anger I'd felt over what I perceived as her complicity in my father's vision for me didn't disappear, it softened. It definitely softened.

Her voice quavered as she went on. "He was angry at first, but I held my ground. When he saw that I wasn't about to budge, he broke down. I'd never seen your father cry before that day—and I never saw him cry in all the years since—but I told him to just let it out, to let it all out, and after he cried himself to the point he couldn't any longer, I asked him the same question I'd hinted at and pushed him toward so many times before: what happened over there in Europe?

"What he told me is what he wrote to you and your brother in those letters. By the time he'd finished, your father was exhausted. Exhausted and ashamed and contrite and about a thousand other things. He'd emptied himself of so much, and I was so glad he had. I also felt something from him that I hadn't felt since before he left for the war. Hope. It was only a glimmer, but it was definitely hope.

"So we talked—the rest of that afternoon, through the chores and milking, into the night, and over the months that followed. It was like we were getting to know each other all over again. Your father was a new man. All the things I'd fallen in love with were still there; maybe they weren't as apparent or they required more effort to tease out. They were there, though. But there was more, too. I knew he'd be carrying a heavy load for the rest of his life, and I knew he'd need me to help him carry it, even if he didn't realize that I would be carrying just as much.

"So I let him do what he had to do to keep living from day to day, year to year. I had to. I wanted to keep my husband."

"His vision for Clay and me." I said.

She nodded. "Don't think it didn't hurt me, too, Walt. But if he was going to survive—if we were going to survive—he needed something to hold on to. I couldn't take that away from him. But he also couldn't take away my hopes." She rose from the chair and sat at the edge of my bed so she could look me in the eye close-up. "And sometimes, prayers do get answered."

I'd been studying my mother as she told her story. I noted the way her eyebrows arched when she spoke with great earnestness, the tremor in her voice when she struggled to maintain control of her emotions, the dirt and berry stains on her hands from working in her gardens and her kitchen. As she spoke, so many things began falling into place: her convincing my father to allow Clay and I special privileges, her leaving my hospital room after my father and Clay had left, her hushed exchange with my father outside my bedroom on the night Clay apologized to me, her conversation with me over lunch after my cast had been removed when she told me it was possible that my father and I could both be right. I embraced my mother and held her more tightly than I ever had.

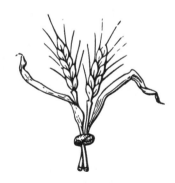

July 2, 1969

TOM HAD CALLED the evening before, and we set a time to get together the next day. At Tom's suggestion, it would be at the Zippel Park ball diamond, and he asked me to bring my glove. I briefly felt the way I had when he told me to come see him after school when I'd handed in my first essay to him Junior year. I'd only known teachers to demand students see them after class when doling out punishment, but Tom had surprised me that day. He'd wanted to compliment me on my work and tell me about the independent study he'd set up for Meg and me. In the two weeks leading up to that after-school meeting, he'd firmly established himself as my favorite teacher, and he cemented the position that day by sharing his belief that words and ideas were more powerful than fists or guns, by telling me my writing possessed a measure of artistry he wanted to help me develop, and by thanking me for sharing my work with him. Now, as I looked forward to meeting with him at Zippel Park, I didn't expect him to surprise me with answers to the questions littering my thoughts; Tom had taught me too well to expect that. Instead, I hoped to surprise myself.

We met in the early evening, after the day's work had been completed on the farm—the second-to-last time I'd milk the cows, as the next day, Clay and I would help our neighbor load the livestock into trailers that would transport them to his farm, just as my parents had wished.

The days were still long, and though our shadows lengthened as we walked to greet each other in the parking lot, we had ample daylight. Tom tucked his mitt beneath his right arm and hugged me as he had on the day of my father's funeral. That first embrace had felt odd, but his genuineness had rapidly swept aside any awkwardness, just as his sincerity had extinguished the strangeness of calling him by his first name or sharing my world with him outside of the classroom.

I asked him how the drive up from Chicago had been, and he said that he and his mother had gone a bit off the beaten path, opting to drive through the countryside whenever possible. "I don't think Mom has ever seen so much green at once in her life," he said. "Concrete and clapboard houses are the old neighborhood."

"I hope she'll like it up here," I said.

"She does already," he said. "But we can talk more about trips and my dear Polish mother another time. On the phone, it sounded like you have some things on your mind. You're looking better than you sounded yesterday."

"Thanks," I said. "I feel better, too."

"Good," he said, slipping his hand into his mitt. "Let's have a catch and talk."

We walked to the high chain-link fence surrounding the diamond and passed through the opening onto the field. We stood in foul territory on the third base side. It was the first time I'd worn my glove in a year, and the first time Tom and I had ever played catch. Having the glove back on my hand, feeling the ball slap into its pocket, and returning the throws reawakened memories. It was a very different dynamic than playing chicken ball with Clay in the side yard at home. Tom had once told me that he'd played some ball in high school, and I could see evidence of that. We didn't talk about playing ball, though—not his past exploits, not my plan to return to the diamond in the Dairyland League next summer. We talked about what I'd gone through over the past two days. And as we sent easy tosses back and forth between us, never increasing the velocity or testing each other's glove skills, I spoke of anger and indignation prompted by my father's letter, the slow unwinding of those emotions in Meg's backyard, only to have them resurface when my mother came to talk to me, and the strangeness of viewing my parents through a new lens as my mother and I rode a roller coaster whose route ended not only with the affirmation of things I'd always suspected about her, but also with a new appreciation for her strength and fortitude and a new understanding of my father.

"Thank God for the energy of youth," Tom said, taking the ball from his glove and throwing it back to me.

"What do you mean?" I asked, returning the throw.

"I'm only seven years older than you, but if I were in your shoes, I don't know that I'd still be upright, let alone slinging the horsehide." Tom slipped off his glove. "Let's take a break," he said.

We went to the bleachers and sat down. We wouldn't have been able to continue playing catch much longer anyway, as the long sunset of midsummer was yielding to a dusk more suited to conversation. "So where are you now?" Tom asked. "Where does this leave you?"

I thought for a long time before I answered, and I appreciated Tom's patience and presence. He was there for me—watchful, but not intrusive; strong, but not overbearing—and when I finally told him I thought I was going to be okay, he simply asked, "What does that mean, Walt?"

I blew out a long breath. "Lots of things," I said. "It means I know now just how much people have cared about me." I looked at Tom and felt my eyebrows raise as my mother's did. "With some, that's been fairly easy to see. With others, it wasn't, but now I know—or know more. I needed that."

Tom smiled and laughed privately. "You brought it, didn't you?" he asked.

I nodded and removed the envelope from my back pocket. "I thought you might—"

"Isn't that something for—"

"No." I cut him off. "I...I need this." I unfolded the letter and apologized for its condition; I'd smoothed it out as best I could after retrieving the balled-up pages from my bedroom floor. "Please."

Tom took the letter and its envelope from me carefully, as though handling something fragile. As he read, I looked around me. From my perch on the bleachers, I could see the loading dock at the rear of Gillett Milling, dusted with the residue of ground corn and oats and waiting for trucks to deliver and pick up their loads in the morning. I could see the rear of Gillett's small police station, an old Chevy police cruiser parked near the door, and wondered if Huggy Bear, the officer who drew overnight duty, would have to hop in and speed to Koeppen's or one of the town's other dozen watering holes to break up a bar fight that night. I could see the clock tower of St. John's Lutheran, my church, pointing skyward, the hour and minute hands creeping northward toward nine o'clock. I thought of the people who would line the parade route in two days—the same people who lined the route each Memorial Day, who filled the bleachers to watch my brother and me play ball, who filled the gymnasium at the high school when I'd graduated more than a year earlier, who filled the pews at St. John's and the four other churches in the city limits. I knew them all, it seemed, and they knew me. It went with living in a small town. That knowledge, I now knew, could only go so far, and as I watched Tom finish reading my father's letter, I wondered what stories those people might have tucked away, what stories they were unable or unwilling to bring to the light of day. I thought of what Twain had written about petrified opinions, something Tom had introduced to me, and though sadness and anger and regret now swirled within me, I also felt myself beginning to understand.

Tom carefully folded the letter and placed it back in its envelope before handing it back to me. "Thank you," he said, his voice low. "That can't have been easy."

"Thanks for the sentiment," I said, recalling how I'd felt when I stormed out the door the night I read the letter, "but it's not just me."

Tom smiled the same smile he did when I'd had epiphanies in his class. "You just proved my point, Walt."

"What do you mean?" I asked.

"A teacher is only successful when he can send his students into the world to tackle problems on their own. Who are you talking about when you say 'it's not just me?'"

I loved him. "My father, my mother, Clay, Meg, this whole town and everyone in it—hell, this whole blasted country."

Tom was beaming. "You know who I've been reading this summer? Sophocles. Most people don't realize that in addition to being a pretty darn good playwright, he was also a general in Athens' army, and when you get past the Oedipus trilogy, his surviving plays are about soldiers who've seen and done terrible things in the name of goodness, things they can't reconcile with their own sense of goodness and what the world had told them was good. And it's not just the soldiers—it's their wives and lovers, the very people for whom they fought and died. Given the drift of things, I thought it couldn't hurt me to do a bit of literary excavation."

Tom could say whatever he wanted about my no longer

needing him as a teacher. Bleachers, food stands, a thick growth of cattails—the world was a classroom for Tom.

"Those characters suffer mightily. Suicides, killing, lashing out when keeping things under wraps can no longer cut it—you name it, they do it, and none of it is pretty."

I thought back to April Fool's Day, remembered the last thing Tyler had said at the Sunroom Café. I'd read *The Poetics* not long after that meeting. "Wasn't Aristotle a big fan of Sophocles?"

"He was," Tom said.

"Tragedies and catharsis—the one can't happen without the other," I said.

"Sharing is good for the soul," Tom said, "and it seems to me, that by listening, you've enabled more than a little catharsis."

Goosebumps rose on my arms.

"Your father is smiling right now," Tom said.

I believed he was right. And I believed that my mother would be able to smile, too. "I only wish…"

"I know," he said. "But that choice was his. He bore his burden in the way that let him live his life, remain true to his vision of a good life and a good family."

"I'm just glad it didn't…" I didn't want to say it.

"Destroy you?"

"Yes," I said, Tom's words giving me license to say it. "Destroy me."

"That's the challenge of living, Walt. Your father, it seems, came to realize some things. I'm merely guessing here, but I'd bet that after writing those letters, he felt different, and likely better."

I thought back to his final year, especially after the doctor had told him I wouldn't be able to serve. The hospital. The hallway outside my bedroom. And, yes, that letter. None of them pleased me, but they all made sense. We hadn't become best buddies, but we hadn't fought, either. Tension was there, but neither of us had taken it as an opportunity to push the other's button. I began to regret his death for new reasons, and I could live with those regrets—perhaps, with time, even embrace them. "I think he did," I said. "And my mom."

"And your mom?" Tom asked.

"Yes," I said. "She's still suffering over his death, but she's found a peace. Her load is so much lighter. Part of it was my injury. Part of it was my dad getting things off his chest, even if that meant stuffing it in an envelope."

Tom pressed his fingertips together. "Maybe with time…"

"I'd like to think that," I said. "Maybe with time, he would have." I paused to consider that statement. I'd never know for certain, but I knew which option I'd favor when considering it late into the night. "And," I said, "I think one last weight was removed from my mother's load, the one that's really brought her peace."

Tom tried to hold back his grin as he spoke. "What's that?"

"Getting her own story off her chest."

We let my comment hang in the air between us. Neither of us spoke as shadows lengthened and daylight was reduced to a thin red line we watched disappear. My eyes had adjusted to the light, and when I looked over to Tom, I saw him rubbing his eyes. "Darn hay fever," he said.

"It's a bugger," I said. "Thank you," I told him. "I needed this."

"You're my friend," he said. "It's what we do." He wiped the palms of his hands down his thighs and leaned over, his elbows positioned just above his knees. "Like me, you're down to one parent. Like I once was, you're about to go out into a big, scary world to carve a place for yourself as the machine tries to chew you up and spit you out. Last question. Teacher to student, but friend to friend, too. I feel like I've had a hand in the man you've become—"

"More than you know, Tom.

"—and I want to know that you're okay."

"Ask away."

"In the face of all this, how can any of us preserve ourselves *and* the ones we love?"

I didn't respond immediately. I thought back over the times we'd shared and what I'd learned from and with and because of Tom, and I smiled. "We stay true to ourselves—"

"Yes."

"—but remain mindful of others—"

"Go on."

"—and we must always share."

"What do you mean by that, Walt?"

"The stories," I said. "They're what keep us alive."

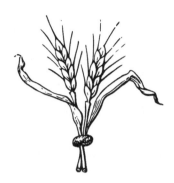

July 3, 1969

CLAY AND I milked the cows for the last time. Our mother insisted on being in the barn with her camera, switching out flash cubes between pictures of us washing the cows' udders, slipping on the black rubber inflations to draw out the milk, dipping the cows' teats in an iodine solution, and pouring milk through a filtered funnel into the large metal cans we toted to cool in the stone tub filled with cold water in the milk house. When she prompted me to smile, I had no difficulty in doing so. I wouldn't miss them. The herd had been good to our family, but with my father gone, Clay leaving for Basic in two days, and my going to Madison in August, selling the cows to a trusted neighbor was the right thing to do.

Clay didn't smile so easily, but then he'd never been the

type to smile for photos. Pictures of him in our mother's album showed the sternest face in America's Dairyland—not angry or sour, just stern. She did capture a hint of a smile in one photo that day when she oohed and ahhed at Clay's muscles as he toted the surge bucket from one of the milking machines.

After milking, we completed the morning chores but didn't herd the cows to pasture; loading them in trailers was easier if we guided them from stanchions to the walled ramp at the barn doors. Melvin Zwijacz and his son Robert, eight years my senior and certain to one day take over his father's operation, arrived soon after the chores.

Though we'd sought to make our job easier by loading from the barn, cows are cows—stubborn, prone to urinating or defecating without warning, massive, and dumbly strong. Not every cow presented a problem; Old Plug lumbered easily, her rear hips swaying slowly, without any prodding. Some, like the young cow we called She-Devil, proved difficult· She-Devil couldn't be milked without positioning a large clamp, resembling an inverted horseshoe with a crank at its axis, in front of her rear hips. Cranked tight, the two halves squeezed to prevent her from kicking. We didn't have the luxury of using the clamp for transport, and she did her best to do everything but what we wanted.

The job took hours. The adult cows were easier to load than the heifers, who hadn't entered the barn since we pastured them in the spring. We collectively worked to close in on each heifer individually, herding it toward the barnyard door. Smaller than the cows, the heifers had spring in their steps. 800 pounds of Holstein trotting toward collision prompted each of us to step out of a heifer's path more than once, requiring us to begin again our efforts to herd the animal into the barn and trailer.

We didn't stop for lunch. By three o'clock, we'd all sweat through our clothes and were covered to varying degrees with chaff, dust, and manure, but with shouts and raised arms, by waving broom handles and pitchforks, we loaded and transported all the cows, 42 adult Holsteins, 24 heifers, and a dozen calves, to their new home. Clay and I stood beneath the light pole near the asphalt shingled well cover. Clay, perched on the edge of the lid, didn't look as tired as I felt. As Melvin spoke with my mother and tucked his check book into his shirt pocket, Robert approached us. "Thank you, guys. Dad and I couldn't have done this alone."

Clay shrugged. "It's what neighbors do," he said.

"Not a problem," I said. "We're happy to help." I wasn't going to miss waking up for 5am milking.

"We'll take good care of them," Robert said. "Your dad had a good herd."

"He did," I said. "He wouldn't have wanted anyone else to have them."

"It's appreciated," Robert said. "I've been hoping to grow our operation for a while now."

I saw an excitement in his eyes I'd never felt and was happy for him.

"If there's anything we can do," Robert said, "to help you out. I know it can't be easy with your mom being—"

Clay interrupted him—not rudely, but coolly, in that way Clay had. "She'll be fine," he said. "We all will. Right, Walt?"

I looked at my brother. "Right," I said. Several of our mother's siblings still lived in Shawano, much closer than either of us would soon be. Peace of mind. "We will."

After the funeral, I'd asked my mother if she wanted me to stay home that fall. She looked at me as if the sun had risen in the west that morning and made it very clear that I wasn't about to abandon my hopes or her prayers for me. She said she hadn't really thought about what she'd now do, but that her gardens always needed tending, that our church would never turn away a volunteer, that the new library might need someone to re-stack the shelves and read for preschoolers at story time, or that she'd discover an adventure waiting for her.

Melvin walked to us. Behind him, dark clouds gathered in the west. "Thank you," he said. "Your father would be proud. You've taken good care of the farm, and we'll take good care of the animals." He shook hands with Clay and me. "Good luck at school, Walt, and Clay, do us all proud. Your father will be smiling down."

"Thanks," I said.

"I will," said Clay.

Melvin and Robert walked to their truck. In their movements, I sensed the same weariness that had settled in my bones.

Mine surpassed the exhaustion of having worked since sunrise, though. If the last three years had beaten me down, the last month had drained me—but not drained enough to dismiss the thought that crossed my mind as we walked toward the house and I looked to the side yard, where the fruit of the cherry trees was just beginning to blush red. "Hey, Clay," I said, "hungry for some chicken?"

"It's been a while," he said, "but you know me."

"I do," I said and went up the front stairs and into the mudroom for our gloves and a baseball.

As we took our places on either end of the yard, the clouds drew closer. Lightning briefly flashed, followed several seconds later by thunder rolling. Clay's first toss was high and lazy, and I could easily see the slow rotation of the red laces as it dropped from the darkening sky. Though tired from the day's work, and though my shoulder was sore from the previous day's game of catch after a year of inactivity, I limbered up quickly. Muscle memory took over. Clay and I had played chicken ball more times than we could count, and for as absurd as the game was, we loved it. Clay and I were so different in so many ways, but this, this we shared; it was my link, however tenuous, to my kid brother.

As we played, I wondered about my brother's reaction to our father's letters. I wasn't surprised that we hadn't spoken of them; it wasn't the only subject floating between us that we couldn't bring ourselves to voice, and I wasn't going to force the issue. My openness with Meg and Tom and even my mother was counterbalanced by the silence between the men in my family. With each other, we'd always been detached. When frustration, desperation, or anger forced a moment to its crisis, we resorted to shouts, resentment, and uneasiness, writhing like something electrical in the hallway outside my bedroom the night Clay offered his apology.

Another step closer.

Clay couldn't have felt what I did when I read my letter. It was impossible. We may have spoken little, but history told me that much. He had his own dreams, and I could only imagine the measure of pride that filled him when he read our father's thoughts about raising us to serve and be better men than him.

Another step. Higher velocity.

He had to be proud, embracing our father's ideals, that he'd become the man our father envisioned when squinting through the mists of time for a glimpse of his sons in the future...

Another. Faster.

... that he—not me—was on the cusp of fulfilling the dream closest to our father's heart, repaying the debt I'd never see as anything but a liability.

Thirty feet. Terminal velocity.

And all that—was okay. We chose targets with impunity. More lightning, more thunder. Clay's next throw was low and hard, a beeline for my right ankle. I speared the ball just above the grass.

I loved Clay. I returned his throw, left shoulder, snapping my wrist for maximum backspin. And it wasn't simply blood. His throw streaked toward my left knee, my mitt swallowing it before it struck me. He was a hell of a ballplayer. Right shin. I wished the scouts had swayed him. I saw Clay as misguided, but his beliefs were his; I wouldn't change them. The knee again. Rain began to fall. I was afraid for him. I knew he'd live through Vietnam, knew that as a soldier he'd carry his body with the same preternatural grace he exhibited on the diamond, treading lightly, gliding through razor grass, over paddy and trail without triggering a mine or allowing an unseen soldier to draw a bead. I threw sidearm, changing the trajectory of the ball, making it rise toward his throat. He snared it with nonchalance. I wasn't afraid for his body. I thought of Tyler. I thought of our father and Wyatt and pleading German soldiers on Crucifix Hill. I feared for his soul.

The rain fell in sheets, but we didn't stop. Our mother called from the porch, but I couldn't hear her voice over the thunder. The knee a third time. I couldn't remember my last win in chicken ball. I might have been nine, maybe ten. A long time ago. I whipped the ball toward his chest, hoping in the act of catching it he'd hear me speak in my throw. *Not a word now. It's okay.* He'd even won years ago when one of my throws had skipped just before reaching him, catching him in the mouth and snapping a front tooth cleanly in half. *But someday.* Angled away from me, I threw at Clay's heel. *You'll talk.* His left hand reached downward, snaring the ball and transferring it to his meat hand as he pirouetted to return the throw. *You'll need to.* I caught the ball a hair's breadth above the bridge of my nose. *And I'll listen.*

As I gripped the ball, the hair on my arms stood on end. A concussion sucked the air from the world for a heartbeat. The butternut tree whose limbs hung over the cows' path to pasture exploded in a flash of smoke and splinters. A thick limb groaned and dropped to the ground, pulling away the bark, exposing a white gash. Our mother screamed, but her voice came from somewhere far away, too far away to reach us. Clay, his smirk situated between amusement and wonder, crouched as he would in the field, motioning for my throw. I hurled the ball, trusting we'd neither flinch nor bail.

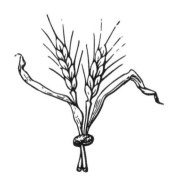

July 4, 1969

I HADN'T SET my alarm as there were no longer cows to milk, but I woke up at dawn anyway. I pulled on a pair of worn jeans and a threadbare shirt that had once been my father's, then sat on the end of the porch to watch the sunrise. I thought of Thoreau and what he'd written about learning to reawaken ourselves with an infinite expectation of the dawn. It was a good thought, and I smiled as I looked out over the yard. The only evidence of the previous day's storm was the tangle of fallen branches and the jagged scar on the trunk of the butternut tree where there'd once been a limb. The cherries were another day closer to picking. Aluminum pie plates tied in the trees with lengths of baler twine discouraged robins from eating the fruit and sounded a faint, tinny chorus in the morning breeze. Across the lane, tall grass lined the banks of the creek that followed a circuitous route before emptying into Spiece Lake.

Meg and I would stop there later in the day on our trip to the meadow. We wouldn't have to worry about my needing to be back for chores or milking or anything else. We were free. The day would be ours.

I sat on the porch as the sun climbed into the sky and heard my mother in the kitchen through the open windows. She'd been the one to end Clay's and my game of chicken ball. She rushed into the yard, the rain soaking her in an instant, and positioned herself between us. Neither Clay nor I wanted to risk beaning our mother, so our contest ended in a draw. I was okay with that, and from Clay's expression, I think he may have been, too. The kitchen sounds painted the picture of what my mother was doing—the sizzle of bacon on the griddle, the crack of egg shells before whites and yolks dropped into a glass bowl, the metallic the whisper of the whisk, the eggs' spitting in a frying pan in melted butter. I heard the refrigerator door, the pouring orange juice, the sudden spring of the toaster trying to eject slices of bread, and the spatula scraping the pan.

My mother came to the porch with my breakfast, and I thanked her. She sat in her chair, an old, worn rocker that had belonged to my grandmother and had been her perch when husking sweet corn or shelling peas. The crisp bacon crumbled between my teeth, leaving the residue of grease and hickory smoke to linger on my tongue. "It's a good day," I said.

"Every day is," she said.

Neither of us spoke as I finished my breakfast. I carried my plate and fork to the kitchen sink, washed and dried and put them away before I went back outside and walked to the machine shed. I pulled the long beaded chain to light the single bulb above my father's workbench. His grindstone was covered by a faint layer of dust, and the acetylene torch and welding mask sat where he'd left them after mending a part for the corn planter that spring. I pulled his chainsaw from a shelf and set it down on the bench to sharpen its teeth as my father had taught me, first nesting the bottom of the bar in the groove cut into a two-foot length of 4 x 4 clamped to the bench, then placing the guide at a 30 degree angle across the top of the bar and fitting the round file I used to sharpen the cutters on the chain with strokes away from me, the rasp of metal on metal telling me I was achieving the desired effect.

I was nearly finished sharpening the saw when Clay came into the shed. "Want a hand?" he asked.

I turned down his offer. "I can handle those tree limbs on my own," I said. "I wouldn't want you to have a run-in with a chainsaw, not with the All-Star Game this afternoon and your leaving tomorrow." He and my mother would soon depart for Sturgeon Bay, as the Door County League was hosting the Door/Dairyland All-Star Game, and none of their teams had a lighted field. My mother had asked that I not go to that game with them, telling me she wanted that time in the car with Clay, a last chance for them to talk about things before he left home.

"I owe you one," Clay said.

I thought of my own last game a year earlier and almost told Clay he didn't, that he'd already paid for a thousand favors from me, but when I thought of our unspoken conversation during our game of chicken ball, I thought better of it. "You do," I said.

Clay and my mother left shortly before 11. I'd already finished cutting the thicker limbs into lengths that would fit our furnace and hauled the rest of the branches and debris to the brush pile on the east end of the empty cow pasture.

I showered and shaved and dressed, waiting for Meg to arrive. I didn't have to wait long. I met her on the gravel driveway as she exited her parents' car. "You look good," she said.

The compliment caught me off-guard, making me momentarily pause before thanking her. It took me a moment to grasp why such benign praise had given me reason to pause: it was the first time since my father's death that she hadn't asked me how I was when we greeted each other. A good thing, I realized.

We gathered our things and began a long, slow walk to the meadow. She was wearing, as always, the agate I'd given her with my promise, and thinking of that day sent a quick, pleasant current through me. I had no presents tucked away for her this day, and I hoped she had none for me, either, as the day and the time and our closeness were presents enough.

I thought of what I'd told my mother earlier in the day when she brought me breakfast on the front porch. We walked down the lane and through the cow pasture, where we remained on the dirt path the animals had beaten, not wanting to step into the grass and any remnants of the pasture's former occupants. We stopped at the culvert through which the creek meandered, where my family piled the rocks that rose with the frost each spring and which we picked from the fields my father had worked. Indian tobacco grew from the edges of the rock pile, its thick stalks covered by the delicate yellow flowers that deposited impossible amounts of pollen if you touched them. A rabbit emerged from the tall grass and quickly ducked into an opening between the stones. A frog, invisible to the eye, nevertheless made his presence known from the banks of the creek where its bank jutted outward, diverting water to slow and swirl before rejoining the current to move toward the lake.

When we arrived at the edge of the pasture, I unhooked the two rubber handled electric fence wires that had served to keep the cows out of the hayfield and functioned as a gate through which tractors and equipment entered the field. Electricity no longer coursed through the wires circling the pasture, and I pulled them off to one side, laying them down in the grass on the edge of the field, leaving the gate open, as it should be.

Meg and I walked through the alfalfa, its thick stems knee-high and just beginning to sprout purple blossoms ahead of cutting the year's second crop. As we crossed the field, it occurred to me that the first time I'd checked the *herrlichkeit* with my grandmother, this field had been planted with alfalfa. I'd been five, and it had nearly reached my waist. Meg and I held hands, as we usually did, and I brought her fingers to my lips to kiss them—her nails extended just beyond her fingertips and were painted a pale pink, and though the skin of her strong hands was soft, it was stained in places by the oil paints she used to paint beautiful canvases. When I'd held my grandmother's hand in my childhood, I'd always been fascinated by the missing segments, the joints she'd lost to a lawnmower but whose absence hadn't diminished their strength.

We passed my deer stand on the northwest corner of the field—I didn't see myself hunting that fall—and made our way to its eastern border and the short path through the aspens and birch to the railroad tracks. We heard the train approaching and waited for it, waving to the engineer perched in the cab of the pilot and watching the long, slow procession of freight cars rumble by. Neither of us grew impatient. The entire day stretched out in front of us.

After the train had passed, we stepped out onto the track and felt its vibration humming in the rails, waiting for it to fade as the train disappeared from sight. We continued walking. The sun was warm on our skin, but not too warm, and the wind passed over us like a whisper. We were walking the same route I'd walked with my grandmother, the sojourn Meg had first and not-so-subtly invited herself to take with me two months shy of three years earlier. We picked flowers. We found pictures in the clouds. We played Pooh sticks at the trestle. We laughed and we smiled easily. It was our day, after all.

When we reached the meadow, we expressed our wonder at the sea of swaying daisies; some things never grew old and never should. We made our way to the spot beneath the beech tree where our blanket had smoothed the bark of its roots as they disappeared into the soil. We ate. We talked. We read poems about good fences and good neighbors, about barbaric yawps and meals equally set, about coy mistresses and fleas and shall I compare thee's, and before we realized it, the sun began to set and the sky to darken. I reached for the one item I'd brought that was new to our collection of essentials, my father's lantern, and lit it. I adjusted the mantle flame to a low glow, and Meg, fishing for a compliment, said something about most women liking low light. I chuckled and gave her what she sought.

We lay on the blanket, our bodies nested together as we felt they should be.

The first stars appeared. We spoke in low voices of our first visit to the meadow, of our two years with Tom, of our parents, and of Clay leaving in the morning. We spoke of my knee, of Meg and my mother and her gardens, of her agate and my painting, of the return trip we'd take to the Apostle Islands later that summer. We spoke of our visit to the meadow the day after graduation, of promises made and of all that had happened.

No signs of daylight remained, and away from town and mercury vapor yard lights, the first few stars had become a twinkling blanket stretched across the sky. After a time, we made love, there beneath the tree on the blanket where we'd first made love and knew we would again. And after that, after limbs reluctantly budging, not wanting to move for fear of letting the warmth of our bodies escape, after we dressed and stood and gathered our things, I adjusted the intensity of the mantle flame. We held each other's hand and let the glow of the lantern light our path home.

Made in the USA
Middletown, DE
08 September 2019